Also Available from Headline Liaison

All of Me by Aurelia Clifford
The Paradise Garden by Aurelia Clifford
The Golden Cage by Aurelia Clifford
Obsession by Catheryn Cooper
The Journal by James Allen
Love Letters by James Allen
The Diary by James Allen
Out of Control by Rebecca Ambrose
Aphrodisia by Rebecca Ambrose
A Private Affair by Carol Anderson
Voluptuous Voyage by Lacey Carlyle
Magnolia Moon by Lacey Carlyle
Vermilion Gates by Lucinda Chester
The Challenge by Lucinda Chester
Hearts on Fire by Tom Crewe and Amber Wells
Sleepless Nights by Tom Crewe and Amber Wells
Dangerous Desires by JJ Duke
Seven Days by JJ Duke
A Scent of Danger by Sarah Hope-Walker
Private Lessons by Cheryl Mildenhall
Intimate Strangers by Cheryl Mildenhall
Dance of Desire by Cheryl Mildenhall

Strangers In The Night

Aurelia Clifford

Copyright © 1996 Aurelia Clifford

The right of Aurelia Clifford to be identified as the Author of the Work has been asserted by her in accordance with the Copyright, Designs and Patents Act 1988.

First published in 1996
by HEADLINE BOOK PUBLISHING

A HEADLINE LIAISON paperback

10 9 8 7 6 5 4 3 2 1

All rights reserved. No part of this publication may be reproduced, stored in a retrieval system, or transmitted, in any form or by any means, without the prior written permission of the publisher, nor be otherwise circulated in any form of binding or cover other than that in which it is published and without a similar condition being imposed on the subsequent purchaser.

All characters in this publication are fictitious and any resemblance to real persons, living or dead, is purely coincidental.

ISBN 0 7472 5165 7

Typeset by
Letterpart Limited, Reigate, Surrey

Printed and bound in Great Britain by
Cox & Wyman Ltd, Reading, Berks

HEADLINE BOOK PUBLISHING
A division of Hodder Headline PLC
338 Euston Road
London NW1 3BH

Strangers In
The Night

Chapter 1

'Coming up to six thirty, and next it's your morning wake-up call with April Sanchez on Mersey Roar . . .'

April glanced at the studio clock as she threw off her jacket and slid into her seat. Almost late. Almost but not quite. Hopefully the studio manager wouldn't have noticed, or she'd be fined for not being in half an hour before her shift. She'd have been here an hour ago if not for Dan Lauren and his insatiable demands . . .

She suppressed a smile as she jammed on the headset and positioned the microphone a few inches in front of her mouth. Through the glass she could see Kieran Harte, the early-morning DJ, feet up on the console and drinking black coffee as he wound down his show. He caught her looking at him and blew her a kiss.

'Piss off, Kieran,' she mouthed and went back to leafing through the running order. Hosting the breakfast show at Mersey Roar FM was a prestige job requiring one hundred per cent concentration. You couldn't ever really relax – turn your back for one moment and there'd be a knife sticking out of it. Well, that was the wonderful world of commercial radio for you.

'. . . That was the Red Hot Chilli Peppers and coming up right after this, someone else who's red hot . . .'

Through the glass, April watched Kieran launch into his lead in to the daily handover. He was good in a slick kind of way, if you liked that sort of thing. Which April definitely didn't, though she supposed some women might be turned on by those broad shoulders and cobalt blue eyes.

'. . . Your chance to wake up with April. And hey, listeners, wouldn't we *all* love to do that . . .'

'Dream on, Kieran,' she muttered under her breath, but she was a professional and she knew how to play the game. When the red light went on and she spoke on-air, it was in her husky, good-morning-let's-fuck voice, the one that brought in a sack of mail every week, half complaining and the other half begging for her telephone number.

'Great gig last night, Kieran?'

'Sure was, April.'

'I heard you got up on stage and jammed with the band.'

'You better believe it. And Jon says you can run your fingers over his Stratocaster any time you like . . .'

She cued up the next two CDs and flicked off the mike. Through the glass partition she could see Kieran packing up in the next studio, stuffing papers into a bag, draining the last drops of coffee from his plastic cup and dropkicking it into the bin. No matter how much he irritated you, you couldn't take your eyes off him.

April sometimes wondered if there was anything about

STRANGERS IN THE NIGHT

Kieran that wasn't a performance. He could be ten different people in the space of ten minutes, but was there a *real* Kieran Harte somewhere in there? From time to time she wished . . . but no, that was stupid. There had never really been anything between them and there never would be. Still, for a split second she caught the look in those blue eyes and had to force herself to turn aside.

Kieran's voice came through on her headphones and she looked up. He was sitting at his desk opposite her, writing labels and sticking them onto the cassettes of magnetic tape which held his latest set of jingles.

'You're looking rough this morning, April. Sexy as hell, but rough. Late night date was it?'

'That's none of your damn business.'

'True. But if you ask me, Dan Lauren's not letting you get enough beauty sleep.'

You didn't go to bed with Dan Lauren to sleep. April hated Kieran for noticing the dark circles under her eyes.

'I hear you made a fool of yourself with a couple of bimbos at the gig last night,' she commented sweetly.

'Says who?'

April tapped the side of her nose.

'You know, Kieran, I'd have thought you'd know better. I mean, if that kind of thing gets back to Marsha . . .'

Kieran chuckled.

'And if she finds out you've been late at the studio three days running . . .'

'Oh, and I suppose you'd be the one to tell her, would you?'

'Come off it, April. I don't need to tell her.'

'Meaning?'

Kieran paused for a moment and sat back in his chair, crossing his feet on the mixing desk. He looked genuinely uncomfortable, but you could never be sure with Kieran Harte.

'Meaning I've been hearing rumours on the grapevine. Apparently there's going to be a big shake up around here.'

'What kind of shake up?'

'I dunno. Nobody tells me anything, I'm just the new boy, remember?' He folded his arms. 'But heads will roll, that's what they're saying.'

'Who . . .?'

April was annoyed with herself for even listening. Kieran was sure to have got it all wrong. He leaned forward so that he was almost touching the glass.

'Coming out with me for that drink tonight, April?'

She tossed her head, shaking out the straggle of coal black waves.

'No.'

'Is that no as in maybe, or no as in yes?'

'It's no, as in I said no yesterday and I'll be saying no again tomorrow, so why don't you just get off my case?'

He grinned. She wished he wouldn't. When he smiled his eyes crinkled at the corners and she almost liked him.

'This could be your last chance.'

'Thank God for that.'

The EMF track was coming to an end and there was no time to get any sense out of Kieran. In any case he was

STRANGERS IN THE NIGHT

getting to his feet and slinging his rucksack over his shoulder.

'See you same time tomorrow then, honeybunch.'

'Not if I see you first, *sweetiepie*.'

The studio door opened and swung slowly shut. The red light above the door lit up: ON-AIR. DO NOT ENTER. April let out her breath in a long, satisfying sigh of relaxation. At last she was alone in her own world, totally confident, totally in control. April Sanchez was the best, nobody would dare dispute that. She opened the mike and leant into it, talking one-to-one into twenty thousand radios.

'Rise and shine, early birds, this is April Sanchez, bringing you breakfast in bed on Mersey Roar, the station that bites back . . .'

It was just after lunch when Marsha Fox called April into her office. April started to feel nervous the moment Marsha switched on the four hundred watt smile. Only praying mantises smiled like Mersey Roar's station manager.

'April, so glad I caught you. I was beginning to think you'd already left.'

April followed her into the office.

'Will this take long? Only I have a meeting with Dan Lauren at Viper Sounds.'

'Oh yes.' The ghost of a frosty smile crossed Marsha's face. 'Dan Lauren. I understand you and he have a rather *special* working relationship.'

'Is that a problem?' April squared up for a fight.

5

'Not at all. The directors are always keen for our DJs to establish solid links with local record companies – as long as it doesn't conflict with their loyalty to Mersey Roar, of course.'

'Do you really think I'm that unprofessional?'

Marsha pointed to a chair and April reluctantly sat down. She'd have preferred to be on eye level with Marsha but the station manager was stalking up and down on her three inch heels in front of the window. It was a dull day and a leaden sky balanced like a sagging grey duvet on the gaptoothed Liverpool skyline.

Marsha swung round to face April, resting her manicured hands on the window sill. She had fast track written all over her, thought April; from the no-nonsense geometric cut of her natural auburn hair through the Catherine Walker two-piece right down to the three hundred pound shoes. Marsha Fox was on the way up, and nothing and no one was going to get in her way.

'You tell me, April. I mean, does a *professional* turn up late for work every day for a week?'

'What?'

'You know the rules, April. If you're not in the studio half an hour before broadcast I have to fine you a day's pay.'

'Oh come on, Marsha, I . . .' Kieran, you conniving bastard, April thought to herself. This is your doing, it has to be.

'Does a *professional* bring in over a hundred letters of complaint a week?'

At this, April's temper flared.

STRANGERS IN THE NIGHT

'Yeah, Marsha – you get a hundred letters complaining and two hundred and fifty telling you how great the breakfast show is. Listening figures for the show have never been so high. Is that some kind of problem?'

'It might be.'

'What!'

'I said it might be. Listening figures aren't the only consideration, April. There's also the question of image . . .'

April looked from herself to Marsha and back again. They couldn't have been more different. April's tousled black mane, black kohl eyeliner and skintight leather jeans tucked into wedge-toed boots were anything but conventional.

'Oh I get it. You don't like the idea of some leather chick presenting your precious breakfast show.'

'The breakfast show is high-profile, April, and we have an image to project. In case you haven't noticed, this station's franchise is up for renewal in six months' time and there are people who don't want it renewed.'

April got slowly to her feet.

'So what are you telling me – smarten up, buy a suit, get my hair cut and quit screwing record-company executives? Because if you are—'

'No. Not that.' Marsha walked across to her desk, pressed a button on her computer and watched a sheet of paper spew out of the laser printer. She tossed it across to April. 'Take a good look at this.'

'What is it?'

'The new programme schedule.'

Aurelia Clifford

April ran her eyes down the columns of print. Even before she spotted her name she had guessed what was about to happen. Guessed, but couldn't accept it, even though it was there in black and white.

'You're . . . no, Marsha, you can't do this. I won't accept it. You can't give Kieran Harte my breakfast show!'

'I can and I am. It's not your breakfast show, April, it's mine, and I'll do as I see fit.'

'It's my show, I developed it, I doubled the audience . . .'

'And we're very grateful for all your hard work. I'm sure Kieran will build on your success. He's—'

'Tame? Slick? Unoriginal?'

'. . . the perfect breakfast DJ. And you're far better suited to the late night audience. I'm sure you'll make the show your own in no time at all.'

April stared at the paper, then at Marsha Fox. There was a cold, sick feeling round her heart.

'The graveyard shift? You're putting me on the all night show? The only show where the presenter outnumbers the listeners?'

Marsha smiled; the glacial, businesslike smile that said I've told you and it's no use arguing, so just get out.

'It's nothing personal, April, it's a business decision. Sven Harlesson broke his ankle doing a Dangerous Sports Club report for the Saturday programme, he'll be in hospital for a few days – and I was intending to move him anyway. We've no one else to take over "Strangers in the Night", and you were the obvious choice. You're the perfect substitute.'

8

STRANGERS IN THE NIGHT

'Substitute! So that's what I am now, is it? A bloody substitute.'

Marsha glanced at the clock, clearly impatient for the conversation to end.

'Look, it's Thursday, why don't you take today and tomorrow off, I'll cover for you. That'll give you plenty of time to prepare for Monday night's show. Oh, and April—'

'What?'

'You will run through the breakfast show with Kieran, won't you? Show him the ropes?'

'There's only one rope I want to show Kieran Harte,' replied April. 'And that's the one I'm going to put round his neck.'

Dan Lauren poured two glasses of brandy and walked across to April. She was sitting crosslegged on his sofa, her legs very long and slim in black boots and leather trousers. The tightest of sleeveless white tee shirts was stretched across her braless breasts, and Dan found himself mesmerised by the way they seemed to quiver and flow with every tiny movement she made.

'Drink?'

She looked up at him and pushed the mass of black hair back from her forehead.

'Thanks. I need it.'

A warm glow of sexual interest made Dan want to rub his crotch. But more than that he longed for the feel of a cool hand on his flame hot sex. April's hand to be precise. He looked at her, lusted after her, had to restrain himself from dragging her onto the carpet and pushing his manhood between her lips.

And what lips, dark and full and slightly parted. Rougenoir lipstick matched the polish on her long, shaped fingernails, highlighting her black hair and pale skin. He wanted her, and he wanted her bad. His bad girl; his streetsmart vampirette.

She took a few sips of brandy and cradled the glass in her hands.

'How could she? How could Marsha do that?'

'It's business, April. These things happen.'

'No.' She shook her head. 'There's more to it than that, it's personal, she's always loathed me. And then there's Kieran Harte . . .'

Dan sat down next to April and took the glass from her, setting it down gently on the coffee table.

'He's not worth bothering about.'

'He's behind this, Dan, I'm sure he is! He's wanted my show ever since he came to Mersey Roar. I'm going to make him pay for this.'

'I told you, April, he's not worth it. Unless . . .'

'Unless what?'

'Unless you've got the hots for him. I know he has for you, it's obvious. Maybe the feeling's mutual.'

'Dan, you're crazy!'

'He's good looking.'

'If you say so.'

'Successful.'

'Not if I've got anything to do with it.'

'Sexy.'

STRANGERS IN THE NIGHT

'What are you, Kieran's agent or something?'

'I'm just trying to find out who it is you're really interested in.'

'But . . .'

'You've talked about nobody but Kieran bloody Harte ever since you got here. All through dinner, the play . . .'

'Sorry.'

She looked up, and her eyes met Dan's. He felt the force of desire sear through both their bodies, knew that she was experiencing it too. It was like a five thousand volt current knifing through their flesh. He pushed a few stray fronds of dark hair off her face.

'Prove it.'

In spite of herself, April found her desire was stronger than her anger. Kieran's face had been the only image in her mind, but now she was looking at Dan, *really* looking at him like it was the first time, and her hunger was electrifyingly intense.

Dan Lauren was a well known figure on the Merseyside music scene. Formerly lead singer with acidhead indie band Outside My Shadow, he had flirted with the art world before setting up his own record company, Viper Sounds. April had met him at a contest for new local bands and something primeval had sparked between them. Dan was unconventionally attractive, powerfully built with a face that was craggy and intriguing rather than handsome, but his aura was darkly sensual and in the few weeks that April had known him, he had become like a drug to her.

'If proof's what you want, darling, proof is what you'll get.'

She took his face in her hands and pulled him towards her, crushing her lips against his, sharing the aftertaste of warm brandy as her tongue pushed its way into his mouth.

His body was hot underneath his shirt, hot with a pulsating warmth which soaked into her as she smoothed her hands down his chest, feeling for the buttons, peeling open his shirt.

Dan reacted by grabbing her by the waist and trying to push her back onto the sofa; but April wriggled free and slipped down onto the floor, tugging his shirt out from his trouser belt and fumbling with the last of the buttons. As she knelt on the floor at his feet, caressing his bare skin, his fingers dived into the dark mass of her hair, raking through it, twisting and caressing it, releasing its flower-scented sweetness.

'Oh April, April baby, have you any idea how good that feels?'

'Of. Course. I. Have', she replied between kisses darted on his bare chest and belly. She stripped away his shirt and dropped it over the back of the sofa. 'But I can do something that feels even better.'

She wriggled deliciously as her fingers unbuckled Dan's leather belt. It felt just as good to be giving pleasure as receiving it. In fact, after the day's unwelcome events, it felt indecently good to be really in control again. And she *was* in control, whatever Dan might think. She had only to touch his bare skin and feel him shudder to know that that was true.

Sliding his belt out of the loops, she discarded it and unfastened the waistband of his trousers. His swollen

STRANGERS IN THE NIGHT

hardness was huge and irresistible beneath his chinos, pushing impatiently against the inside of his zipper and distending it into an arching metal centipede.

Rather than simply sliding down the zip, April ran her fingernails over the fat bulge of her lover's penis, tracing its outline, moving slowly from base to tip, again and again stopping just short of the painfully sensitive glans beneath the thin material.

'Bitch,' breathed Dan, eyes closed and breathing heavily.

It was an expression of love and admiration. He'd had plenty of women, but few of them had reduced him to this level of ecstatic passivity. Normally he liked to be the aggressor in sex, the predator, but right now he was quite happy to just sit back and let April Sanchez have her wicked way with him.

Still touching him through his pants, April took the long, thick rod of flesh between her fingers and began rubbing it; not hard enough to risk moving things along too quickly, but with enough skill to make Dan grunt and groan and shift his backside at each stroke of her fingers. She had still not touched his glans, and a tiny patch of wetness showed as a dark stain on the pale beige linen.

He was excited. Really excited. And that made April hungrier than ever for him. Did he guess that she was soaking wet between her thighs? That inside those black leather jeans her panties were little more than a twist of wet lace, pushed up hard between the petals of her sex?

Bending lower over her conquest, April parted her lips.

13

The matt rouge-noir lipstick would leave a stain, but who cared? Certainly not Dan. He was lying back, eyes closed, breathing hard and fast. The beating of her own heart raced even faster as she moulded her lips to the damp swell which marked the juicy plum of his cock tip.

Her breath was steamy and hot as she teased him gently with her teeth and breathed hard, forcing the warm air through the fabric. She could taste the scent of him through his pants, anticipated the tang of his sex on her tongue, the slippery wetness which would ooze and trickle between her lips and slide down her throat.

Her fingers slipped down to the twin swell of his balls, taut and hard and ready for her. Her index finger, tipped by a talon the colour of dried oxblood, slid between Dan's parted thighs and traced the deep roadway between his anus and the root of prick and balls. He flinched, moaned and pushed her face harder against his crotch.

'You'll make me spurt,' he whispered. 'Without even touching me.'

April giggled. She was high on the power of sex, on the muted taste of Dan's pleasure as it seeped through his pants. It had been a bad day, but it was getting better.

'I want you,' he said abruptly, opening his eyes and making her raise her head. A perfect lipstick outline marked the kiss of her dark red lips on his still veiled dick. 'I have to unzip this, April, before you drive me crazy.'

His fingers trembled slightly as they drew down the tag and the zipper gaped open. Lifting his backside from the sofa, he drew down his chinos and kicked them off. He

STRANGERS IN THE NIGHT

smiled at the look of undisguised lust on April's face.

'Still like it?'

She traced the smoothness of the metal ring with the very tip of her finger. It passed neatly through the head of Dan's penis, entering through the single tiny eye and emerging at the base of the glans.

'Every time I see this, I've forgotten just how beautiful it is. Tell me again how it feels. To have a pierced dick.'

'You wouldn't believe it. It's better than any drug I've ever taken.'

'You weren't . . . afraid?'

Dan laughed.

'April darling, what is there to be afraid of but pain? And since pain is only another form of pleasure . . .' He lowered his voice and cupped April's breasts in his hands, savouring their firmness. 'You know . . . I've often thought that I'd love to see you pierced.'

'My nipples?'

'Nipples, navel, labia.' He paused. 'Forget tattooing, this is the only form of body art that gives real pleasure. How about I pay for you to have your clit done? They say it's incredible, after you've had it done the sensations are a hundred times stronger . . .'

'Maybe.' A cold shiver of excitement raised the hairs on the back of April's neck. 'I don't know if I could.'

'A woman like you can do anything she wants. Anything she puts her mind to.'

April put out her tongue and tasted the cockring. It was real gold, eighteen carat at least, seasoned with the elixir of Dan's pleasure, salty and strong. She'd never really

15

flirted with the idea of piercing, but she found Dan's cockring incredibly arousing.

'Why don't you take it in your mouth?'

His words echoed her desire. Her saliva was welling up in anticipation of the delicious taste of pierced dick on her tongue. Her lips encircled Dan's cocktip, engulfed it, slid down the stiff shaft until its tip was bumping against the back of her throat.

'Mmm. Oh yes, April, you're good, really gooood.'

She cupped Dan's balls in her hands and squeezed gently, in the way that she knew drove him into an insanity of pleasure. His shaft was iron-stiff and the cockring was warm on her tongue, turning round and round and round in her mouth, filling it up, making her want not just to lick and suck but to bite and devour . . .

Just when she was certain that Dan was about to come, he withdrew from her lips. He was bigger and harder than she ever remembered him being, obviously on the very brink of orgasm.

'Dan, why won't you let me . . .?'

'Because I want you to feel this way too, that's why. Oh God, April, I have to taste you. I can smell you, do you know that? I want to taste you and I want to see you in rubber and chains . . .'

He lowered her to her belly on the floor and, reaching underneath her, unfastened her trousers, easing the skintight leather down over the hard swell of her backside. Underneath she was wearing only the briefest of knickers, the lace gusset turned to a wet rag by her pleasure and pushed hard into the haven between her

STRANGERS IN THE NIGHT

outer labia, tormenting her with surges and ripples of sensation.

'Beautiful,' he murmured, pulling her up until she was on her hands and knees. He was behind her and her hair was hanging down in front of her face in a midnight black cascade. She could see nothing, only hear the sex in his voice and feel his hot hands caressing her body.

Something sharp bit into the smooth curve of her buttock and she realised that Dan was nipping her with his teeth, smothering her with wet kisses that left trails and pools of cooling saliva all over her skin. His fingers were busy, busy, busy; scratching and stroking and now rubbing, using the twisted lace of her panties to tease her eager flesh.

Her pussy was an ocean of wetness, and she growled softly, offering herself up to the pleasure. The gusset of her knickers was hard and scratchy, and Dan was relentless in his quest to torment her. He was rubbing it back and forth with a sawing motion, forcing it deeper into the softness of her sex, drawing it roughly across the hidden pout of her anus and the hard pink stalk of her desire.

'I want you, I want you, I want you,' she moaned to the rhythm of Dan's caresses. Her backside tingled and stung from the sharpness of his bites, the skin tight and shivering from the cold trickles of his saliva.

Dan's finger slipped underneath the centre line of April's panties, pushing the gusset aside. Cool air licked and kissed the moist flesh beneath, making April sway her hips from side to side in delight. Dan's fingernail skated along the inner margin of her sex, tracing the concentric

17

Aurelia Clifford

frills of dark pink flesh, moving closer but oh so slowly towards the stonehard button of her clit.

She knew how it would feel when he touched her there, but the anticipation could not prepare her for the convulsive shudders of excitement which shook her body as one finger, two, then three, entered her and began to twist and push and rotate.

'Ah. Ah. Ah.'

Her breath escaped in short gasps and she panted like a bitch in heat, pushing out her backside to take in more, more, more. When Dan's tongue made contact with her clitoris she almost screamed her pleasure, certain that he must make her come instantly.

But Dan Lauren knew a lot about women. Enough to keep a lover on the edge of ecstasy almost indefinitely. And tonight he planned to keep April Sanchez simmering on the hotplate for a long, long time before tumbling with her into the furnace heat of orgasm.

The following Monday night found April sitting alone in Studio 2 at Mersey Roar.

It was late. She could have been at a post-gig party, or a late night film screening ... or playing bedtime games with Daniel Lauren. Instead of which she was here, in an almost deserted radio station, thumbing through a playlist which looked like the passenger manifest from the *Titanic*. The Doors, Lennon, Hendrix, Lynyrd Skynyrd, Marvin Gaye, Elvis ... "Strangers in the Night"? "Seance in the Night", more like. She wondered if the audience were all dead too.

STRANGERS IN THE NIGHT

She faded down a wailing blues anthem and turned to the switchboard at her elbow. Green lights were flashing on and off. She flicked a switch and made love to the mike.

'That was Janis Joplin, now let's change the tempo, get down and mellow out. Who's that on line five?'

'You can call me Max.' The voice was smooth, agreeably sensual.

'OK Max, what do you want to talk about tonight?'

As he replied, she knew he was smiling.

'I want to talk . . . about sex.'

April's finger hovered over the button that would cut him off and cast him adrift. Her instructions had been clear: no smut, no pervs, nothing the directors and the old ladies could object to. But then again, how many directors and old age pensioners were listening at two in the morning?

'Really?'

'Really.' His voice was hardly more than a whisper. 'You have a sexy voice, April.'

She ought to cut him off, she knew she ought . . .

'I'd like to touch you, April. And kiss your hair. I love stroking long hair and using it to caress my body, don't you, April? I'd like to tell you . . . about my fantasies . . .'

April glanced down at the switchboard, then snatched her hand away and, picking up the playlist, ripped it straight down the middle and threw it into the bin. Fuck Hendrix. Fuck Jim Morrison and the Beach Boys. If Marsha Fox was making her dig up this corpse of a show she'd be doing it her own way. And she was going to begin

19

the resurrection by injecting a few milligrammes of danger.

'April . . . are you still listening?'

'Sure I'm listening, Max. We're *all* listening. Now, why don't you tell us all about those secret fantasies of yours?'

Chapter 2

'Gonna touch down, blast off, power up my astral sex machine . . . sex machine . . . sex machine . . .'

The song disintegrated into a hypnotic blur of synthesisers and distorted guitars and April Sanchez's voice faded up, teasingly sweet and low.

'It's coming up to four o'clock and dawn's breaking over the big city. Time for bed, night owls. This is April Sanchez with a goodnight kiss, and a little something to sing all you intimate strangers to sleep . . .'

She slid the CD into the slot and selected track twelve. Chris de Burgh; that ought to be comatose enough to fool any early early birds who might be listening in to check up on her – like Marsha Fox, for example. April smiled. As yet, Marsha might be completely unaware of what was happening to "Strangers in the Night", but the night owls knew exactly where April Sanchez was coming from . . . though sometimes she wished she didn't know what some of *them* were up to.

The new early morning DJ in the next studio was babbling about some inane 'phone-in competition when April gathered up her stuff and left. The building was in semi-darkness, only the dim nightlights glowing on the stairwell and nobody on reception to hand out car stickers and baseball caps. Maybe working in the middle of the night wasn't so bad after all.

She'd lied about the dawn. It was pitch black outside, not so much a city as a series of dark canyons, illuminated by parallel lines of tired sodium moons. It was quite cold too. Perhaps she should have brought a jacket. The damp chill seemed to cling to her bare arms and throat, turning smooth skin to gooseflesh and turning the soft discs of her nipples into hard nodules which were clearly visible through her sleeveless tee shirt.

Unlocking her car, she slipped into the driving seat and switched on the ignition. As she steered out onto the main road the radio blared into life.

'. . . Nervous, Sophie?'

Sophie giggled. 'Yeah. A bit . . .'

'A bit, *Uncle Neil*.'

'Yeah, right, Uncle Neil.'

'OK Sophie, let's see if you can guess what's in Uncle Neil's Big Box for an electric juicer and a Mersey Roar funbag . . .'

That's quite enough of that, thought April, mentally consigning "Uncle" Neil Fellowes to the deepest pit of hell as she clicked off the switch. If Marsha Fox had her way, they'd all be like Neil: glib, unfunny, plastic injection moulded DJs for a plastic generation.

She drove for a while through the city streets, empty save for the odd wino and stray clubber, too late to go

STRANGERS IN THE NIGHT

home, too early to go to work. As she turned right and headed towards the Mersey Tunnel she glanced in the rearview mirror and noticed that a car behind her was turning right too. Funny that; she could have sworn that same car had been on her tail as she drove away from Mersey Roar. You didn't get many dark blue Lancias in the middle of Liverpool.

Then again, she might have been imagining it. She took a left, then drove straight on into the mouth of the tunnel. Soon be home; another twenty minutes or so, and she'd be turning on the shower, washing away the shadows.

That car – it was still there, staying the same distance behind her, unable to overtake in the tunnel. April watched it in her mirror. She couldn't make out the driver's face, only the dark shape of a single figure in the car. A man's silhouette. Someone was following her, some crazyhead who'd been listening to the show. She'd been wondering when the weirdos would start coming out of the woodwork, and now it was starting to happen.

April's heart was pounding but she fought to stay calm. Whatever else she did, she mustn't drive straight home: that would only let him know where she lived. If he wanted a mystery tour, that was exactly what he was going to get.

As they emerged from the tunnel onto the Birkenhead side, she sped across the flyover, hit the brakes and swung right. Sure enough, the blue Lancia followed as though it was stuck to her back bumper with superglue. If this went on much longer, they'd end up in Chester. Right, left, left

Aurelia Clifford

again, they were going in circles through the same dock-side streets, covering the same ground again and again. When would he get tired of this game and give up?

He was gaining on her. She hadn't noticed at first, but he was definitely getting closer. For the first time she began to be seriously worried. The Lancia was far more powerful than her ageing Nissan, it was useless trying to outrun it. Maybe she ought to drive back into Liverpool or head for the nearest police station?

They were approaching a vast piece of overgrown waste ground, where several blocks of back-to-backs had been demolished to make way for some megaplex shopping development that had never happened. On impulse, April drove straight onto it, suspension creaking as the tyres bounced on shattered bricks and old bedsprings. A sharp turn and she was heading back the way she'd come, driving head on into the headlights of the oncoming Lancia.

How she kept her nerve, she had no idea. Afterwards it was all a blur. She had her foot down, she was driving straight for the Lancia, daring it to keep on coming.

At the very last moment the driver swung off right and plunged, bonnet first, into a shallow ditch at the edge of the demolition site, wheels locking in soft mud. April parked up and jumped out, grabbing a tyre lever just in case of trouble.

'Get out. Go on, get out!'

She hammered on the side of the driver's door. It opened and the driver stepped out, perfectly calm. Smiling even.

'What the hell . . .?'

STRANGERS IN THE NIGHT

Dan Lauren brushed imaginary creases from his shirt sleeve.

'I was beginning to think I'd never catch up with you.'

April's hand fell to her side, the tyre lever dangling uselessly.

'Dan. What the fuck do you think you're playing at?'

He looked genuinely surprised.

'Did I scare you, April? I enjoy a chase – don't you?'

He reached out and stroked April's cheek. She seized his hand and wrenched it away.

'Don't you bloody touch me, you bastard.'

Dan's lips brushed the back of her hand.

'You should get angry more often, it suits you. It makes you smell . . . exciting.'

'Why were you following me?'

Dan leaned back against the side of his car.

'You've made a bit of a mess of the Lancia,' he observed casually. 'I only bought it last week, too.'

'I said *why*, Dan?'

'You're a very exciting woman, April. More exciting even than I'd realised. I couldn't sleep, so I decided to give your late night show a try.'

'You were listening in?'

Dan's hands reached out and prised the tyre lever from April's fingers, dropping it onto the ground.

'I should have listened sooner. I had no idea it was so . . . arousing. Have you any idea what it does to me, April, listening to you talking like that on the air? To complete strangers? God alone knows what it does to them . . .'

25

Aurelia Clifford

'You followed me all the way out here just to tell me that?'

'Naturally.'

'You frightened the life out of me, just to tell me that you've got the hots for me? You're crazy, Dan.'

'That's what you do to me.'

Half angry with Dan, half confused by the delicious sensation of his fingers on her bare throat, she turned away. But Dan took hold of her and made her meet his gaze. His eyes were dark, glittery, relentless in their pursuit of pleasure.

'Look at me, April. And tell me you don't want me too.'

She spat back her reply, but they both knew she was bluffing.

'Don't flatter yourself, Dan. I don't need this kind of shit.'

'But you need me. Don't you, April?'

This time his hands slipped down from her throat to her breasts, and cupped them very gently. Her nipples, already hardened by the cold night air, slipped treacherously easily into the niche between thumb and index finger.

'Dan. Don't . . .' she breathed, but her inner self was urging do, do, do it to me. Do it to me again and again, and when I scream at you to stop, do it some more.

Squashing April's breasts together with his left hand, Dan stooped to take both nipples into his mouth, warming them with his breath, moistening and biting them through her tee shirt. She moaned and halfheartedly pushed him away, but his right hand was already pushing up her leather miniskirt and sliding up her thigh.

STRANGERS IN THE NIGHT

She was wearing hold-up stockings and a stretch thong, so tiny that it barely veiled her sex and completely exposed the magnificent swell of her buttocks. Dan's hot palm smoothed over and over the bare flesh, lightly and yet purposefully.

'You're incredible, April. Incredible. I want you. I want this beautiful body . . .'

'If you want me, you'll have to take me.'

That was what she wanted, she realised with a shock. For Dan to take her roughly, strip her and have her and force the pleasure from her all too willing body.

Dan took her by the shoulders, swung her round and pushed her across the bonnet of the Lancia. It was still warm from the engine, and its heat soaked into her back through the thin cotton of her tee shirt, contrasting with the chill night breeze blowing across her bare skin.

'This is what you love, isn't it, April? To be my plaything.'

She wanted to deny it, but they both knew she would have been lying. It was strange how submissive she found herself becoming when Dan Lauren awoke the hunger in her belly. Normally she was sexually adventurous, aggressive even; but with Dan she was a mindless toy, a creature dominated by the sensations he wove in a net above and in and through her body.

'Give it to me, Dan. Give it to me now.'

Hot, dry hands pushed up her tee shirt, exposing her breasts. They were small and firm, apple round even when she was lying on her back; the nipples turned to stalks of shameless lust. Dan kneaded them like bread dough,

Aurelia Clifford

squeezing and stroking, flattening and erecting them, alternately causing her discomfort and intense delight.

His thigh pushed between her legs and they parted for him, offering him the secret of her sex. Her leather skirt was high on her thighs, baring the base of her belly and the clipped triangle of her pubic hair, a dark and glossy chestnut in contrast to the jet black waves spread across the car bonnet.

Hot flesh on cool flesh. Dan's hands began just above her knees and moved slowly, slowly, slowly up towards the apex of her pubis. She throbbed for him, ached and hungered and thirsted. She hated herself for her weakness but Dan Lauren *was* her weakness, an irresistible urge it would be madness to resist.

As his fingers opened her up, a hot gush of liquid escaped from her; she felt it trickle out of her sex, oozing and dripping down the deep furrow to her anus, forming a pool on the warm metal beneath her backside.

'You're hot for me, April. As hot as I am for you.'

He did not push his tongue into her or tease her clitoris with light caresses of his fingertips, though she moaned softly and rubbed her backside back and forth, desperately trying to make him give her the pleasures she craved. This time, Dan Lauren was too hungry to care about anything but his own need. His need to be inside her.

His pierced cock tip nuzzled briefly into the deep well of her inner sex, hesitating at its entrance, teasing and sliding over the sweet abundant slick of wetness, glancing over the exposed head of her swollen clitoris.

It was hell and it was heaven. The expectation was the

STRANGERS IN THE NIGHT

worst part of it, the not knowing when and if he would fill the aching emptiness of her sex. What if he left her like this? What if he satisfied himself by simply rubbing the tip of his cock between her pussy lips, never lingering on her clitoris long enough to bring her to orgasm, spurting over her belly and leaving her to plead with him to end the pain?

The sudden, scything movement of his dick between her thighs drove all the breath from her in an explosive grunt. She felt the car's suspension judder and dip, and her body moved with it, pushed down and then exploding back up to meet the force of her lover's thrusts.

Belly to belly, she ground against the hardness of bone and muscle, eating him up, sucking him into her, wanting more and more and still more. Her fingers clawed at his back, pulling him in closer, making his thrusts deeper and harder. Her body was singing with exhilaration, vibrating with pleasure, quivering closer and closer to the point of no return.

She opened her eyes and looked up. Dan's face was above her but it was silhouetted against the orange halo of a street light, making him look like some unholy, featureless angel, dark and relentless; a mechanical lover of polished and blackened steel.

'Yes, yes, *YES*!'

It ended in fireworks, an explosion of light and pleasure, a wet heaven of satisfied lust. And then, as the first bluish smudge of dawn highlighted the horizon, it began all over again.

★ ★ ★

Aurelia Clifford

Time passed. Two weeks, three, and still no one at Mersey Roar had questioned what April Sanchez was doing with the night time show. In all probability they hadn't even bothered listening to it. Well, that suited April down to the ground. As long as her listeners kept on tuning in, as long as she could do what she damn well liked, that was all that mattered.

Some nights went well, others less so. But there were more good nights than bad. It seemed Merseyside wasn't short on insomniacs who wanted to talk about life, love, sex and fantasy. It made great listening. April knew that. Although she'd have been the last to admit it, 'Strangers in the Night' was beginning to turn her on; taking hold of her and becoming a curiously sensual obsession, like having sex with a stranger and never even seeing his face.

About three a.m., with the show in full swing and the switchboard flashing like Blackpool Illuminations, April was startled by a voice coming over on her headset.

'You have the cutest backside, April. Has anyone ever told you that?'

'W-what?'

She craned her head round but there was no one there. The 'phone lines weren't open and she checked the mike; it was closed too. At least the listeners hadn't heard it over the top of the music. She went on cueing up the next three tracks.

'I bet you'd look terrific in PVC.'

This time she swivelled right round in her chair. She could have sworn she made out a shape in the darkened doorway.

30

STRANGERS IN THE NIGHT

'Who is this? Is this some kind of joke?'

'Long time no see, April. Haven't you missed me?'

A shape moved forward out of the shadows. *Now* she knew. She let out a gasp of irritation.

'Kieran Harte, you scumbag. What are you doing here?'

Kieran strolled into the studio, hands in the pockets of his white denims. He looked . . . annoyingly good. Obviously fronting the breakfast show, *her* breakfast show, suited him. His sandy hair was trendily short with a floppy fringe that slipped from time to time over one blue eye, giving him the air of a naughty schoolboy. He was good looking, was Kieran Harte, thought April. And he was a bastard. A rotten, conniving, doubledealing bastard.

'Thought I should come and re-establish diplomatic relations.'

'*What*?'

'It's good. The show. You're making a great job of it.'

'Oh really?' April's voice was heavy with sarcasm. 'And it's all thanks to you, isn't it? I mean, if it hadn't been for you I'd never have had the chance to take on the graveyard shift, now would I?'

Kieran didn't even have the good grace to look ashamed. He came and perched on the desk beside her.

'I know you blame me for what's happened . . .'

April treated him to a hard stare. Squirm, you bastard, she willed him. He kept on smiling.

'Too right I do. If you hadn't told Marsha Fox . . .'

'I didn't.'

You—?'

'I didn't tell her anything. She and I . . . don't see eye to

31

eye, never have since I joined the station. To be honest, I was as surprised as you were when she gave me the breakfast show.'

'Didn't turn it down though, did you?'

'Hold on, April. I mean, would you have turned down a chance like that?'

'That's hardly the point.'

'Maybe. But that doesn't alter the fact that I didn't have anything to do with Marsha's decision. And I certainly haven't been badmouthing you to her.'

'Pull the other one, Kieran.'

'I'm telling you the truth, April.'

Kieran placed his hand on April's. It was a small gesture, but it stopped her in her tracks. It was several seconds before she pulled away, and even then she avoided his gaze.

'If you say so.'

'I do. Cross my heart and hope to die.' He drew his finger across his chest.

'OK, just supposing I do decide to believe you – why have you come here tonight? To gloat?'

'To make peace. To persuade you to have that drink with me. And I suppose . . .' His words dried in his throat. April made herself look into those deep blue eyes, those eyes that threatened not to let her escape.

'And what?'

'It's just . . . look, I'm not very good at this, but . . . I've been listening to your show, April, and it's great, only . . . only I think you should be careful.'

It was two nights later and the show was in full swing. The

STRANGERS IN THE NIGHT

crazies were really coming out of the woodwork tonight, and that was just how April liked it.

'OK. So let me get this straight. You say Lee Harvey Oswald was a Freemason?'

'That's right.' The voice on the other end of the line was squeaky with excitement. 'It all makes perfect sense, don't you see?'

'Yeah, right, well that's really interesting. Thank you and goodnight, Chris from Prescot. Now I think we have another caller on line two . . .'

She pressed down the switch and cut off Chris in mid-flow. She had an underwear fetishist on line four but she was saving him for later.

'Line two? This is Mersey Roar and tonight we're talking about passion. Are you there, caller? Hello?'

There was a long silence. She was about to move to the next record when a man's voice cut in. It was deep, slow, slightly muffled.

'What do you listen to when you make love, April? I think I know.'

This was more like it. Spooky but sexy, the kind of conversation the listeners liked to hear. April decided to play him along for a while.

'What's your name, caller?'

'That's not important. I want to talk about you. I want you to tell me about yourself, April.'

'I'm sure we'd rather hear about you . . .'

'You wear black silk panties, don't you April? Black silk with lace edging. They're tight, and the centre seam rubs you when you wriggle your backside on your chair. You

33

could bring yourself off like that, April, have you ever tried it? Why don't you try it right now, while I listen?'

April kind of wanted to laugh. After all the guy was clearly cracked. But something about his voice was chillingly serious, unpleasantly compelling.

'We're talking about passion, caller. Do you have a passion you'd like to tell us about?'

'My passion is you, April. Dedicate the next record to me – it's *Hold me, Thrill me, Kiss me, Kill me*, isn't it? Good night, April. I'll be dreaming of you.'

April heard the distant click of the 'phone receiver and then several seconds' silence. The frantic flickering of green lights on the switchboard brought her back to reality.

'We'll be back with another secret passion right after this.'

As she faded up the next song she glanced at the CD case lying on the console in front of her. U2: *Hold me, Thrill me, Kiss me, Kill me*. How could he possibly have known?

Chapter 3

Having lunch with Marsha Fox was a little like having lunch with a piranha fish.

Still, an invitation from Marsha was a rare occurrence and you quickly learned never to say no. Besides, since the schedules had been turned upside down it was even rarer for April Sanchez to see daylight. No, the invitation itself wasn't the problem; what bothered April was *why*.

'Nice restaurant,' she commented as a waiter topped up her wine glass. 'Food's good, too.'

Marsha's eyes travelled up from the floor, covering every inch of the waiter's six-four frame.

'I don't come here for the food, darling,' she said, reluctantly tearing her gaze away from the waiter's retreating backside. 'Know what I mean?'

'I guess.' April gave the waiter a passing glance. He was Hollywood Man personified, six foot four of chargrilled hunk, lightly toasted for that authentic West Coast flavour. His perfect golden tan looked as if it had been rolled in olive oil – which was probably what Marsha Fox would like him to do to her. 'He's not really my type.'

Aurelia Clifford

'Ah yes.' Marsha's meticulously-painted lips twitched at the corners. 'So who *is* your type, April?'

'You don't want to hear about my sex life', countered April.

'Oh I don't know, maybe I do. Maybe I want to hear all those sexy things you get up to with Daniel Lauren. You know, really and truly I'd have thought he was a little . . . raw, even by your standards.'

April's eyes flashed danger but Marsha wasn't taking any notice.

'What I do in my own time is my own business.'

'I suppose so.' Marsha picked at something expensive wrapped in filo pastry. 'Up to a point.'

'And what is that supposed to mean?'

'Only that you're our product, April darling. Whatever you do, wherever you do it and with whom, it reflects on the station. And as a matter of fact I have something planned for you . . .'

Alarm bells sounded inside April's head.

'The last thing you planned landed me on the graveyard shift. So thanks, but no thanks.'

Marsha's brown eyes sparkled with the joy of being in control.

'This one's not optional, sweetie. We're having an open day at Mersey Roar next week, for the local kids . . .'

'No, Marsha. Absolutely not.'

'You'll be brilliant, I know you will. Sign a few autographs, help the brats make their own radio show . . .'

'Get Kieran to do it. He did it last year, he can do it again.'

STRANGERS IN THE NIGHT

'Kieran's busy, darling.' Marsha's smile was full of smug self-congratulation. 'He has a breakfast show to present.'

April threw down her fork in disgust.

'Is that why you asked me here, to humiliate me?'

'Not at all.' To April's surprise, Marsha reached over and began stroking the back of her hand. 'You have beautiful skin, April, has anyone ever told you that? Beautifully smooth. I'd hate anything to happen to it . . .'

April's eyes widened. She drew her hand away.

'Was there something else you wanted to talk to me about?'

'You're not afraid of me, are you, April?'

Marsha's voice was a kitten's purr, soft and seductive. April's mouth was dry. She wanted to swallow, but there was a hard lump in her throat and the palms of her hands felt sticky with sweat. She picked up her serviette and wiped her fingers.

'Why should I be afraid of you?'

'Because I'm . . . powerful? After all, your career is completely under my control.' As though the gesture had nothing to do with what she was saying, Marsha casually picked up a sesame breadstick and snapped it in two. 'If your performance doesn't come up to my very high standards, well . . . but I'm sure it won't come to that, will it, April?'

Marsha's tongue licked slowly round her lips, picking up a few stray crumbs and taking them into the dark wetness of her mouth.

'You can't intimidate me, Marsha.'

37

Aurelia Clifford

Yes she can, whispered a treacherous voice inside April's head. Yes she can, and yes she does, and something deep inside you quite likes the feeling. It wasn't Marsha's words which unsettled April, it was a different kind of power. A sensual awareness, an aura of seductive energy which threatened to draw her into it and engulf her.

'Of course not.' Marsha sipped chilled Muscadet, her long fingernails tapping lightly on the bowl of the glass. 'But I can make you *do* things, can't I? I mean, no one wants to lose their job, do they? Not for the sake of some stupid principle.'

April forced herself to take a bite of marinated chicken, chew it and swallow it. Her silence clearly irritated Marsha.

'Aren't you going to ask me what I mean?'

'I'm sure you'll tell me if I wait long enough.'

'The thing is, April, I've just received the audience figures for last month.' She took a sheet of paper out of her briefcase and laid it on the table. 'Kieran's breakfast show is doing quite well, I'm sure you'll be pleased to know that.'

'Better than *my* breakfast show?'

Marsha ignored the question and went on.

'We've decided to give him the weekend breakfast show as well. Sven's making a pretty good job of the drivetime slot, and Mike Meen's "Battle of the Bands" is picking up new listeners every week . . .'

'And *my* show? What about "Strangers in the Night"?'

Marsha turned the sheet of paper and pushed it across the table to April.

STRANGERS IN THE NIGHT

'Your audience is up forty three per cent, April. *Forty three per cent*. Congratulations.'

April searched Marsha's face. There was not a trace of a smile on those dark ruby lips.

'Why do I get the feeling I'm being criticised?'

Marsha leaned across the table until her face was uncomfortably close to April's.

'I don't know what it is you're doing, April, but somehow you're raising the dead from their coffins and getting them to tune in to Mersey Roar. I don't think either of us wants me to know what that something is.'

April braved out the hard stare.

'I'm a good DJ. A professional, you know that.'

'Maybe. But let me make one thing clear, April. If you value your job and you want to keep it, you'll be careful.'

'Are you threatening me?'

'I wouldn't do a thing like that.' Behind her smile, Marsha's teeth were glossy white and razor sharp. 'All I'm saying is, do what you're told and don't let your show become so popular that I have to tune in. Is that perfectly clear?'

The Mersey Roar Charity Open Day came and went. It was an experience April preferred to forget. Nursemaiding a dozen delinquent girls from the local detention centre wasn't her idea of a fun afternoon – neither had it turned out to be theirs, as most of them had only agreed to come because they wanted Kieran Harte's autograph.

Kieran. Bloody Kieran. That name followed her everywhere, drove her crazy, made her so paranoid that she half

39

Aurelia Clifford

believed that no matter what she achieved, no matter what fantastic opportunities she made for herself, she'd turn her back for a moment and Kieran Harte would have strolled in and taken them for himself.

The worst thing was not being able to hate him. Oh, she resented him, sure she did. Mistrusted him even. He was a thorn in her side and there were times when she'd have liked to wring his neck. But there was something about him . . . something disarming, something annoyingly sexy too. He could drive her mad, but always when she tried to square up to him and confront him, she ended up wondering what it would be like to have him in her bed.

It was only half an hour to midnight when she pushed open the front door and walked into Reception. Soraya from Bhangra Beat was leaning on the desk talking to Sherrie the receptionist, who was putting on her coat ready to leave. Already most of the lights had been switched off and the station was subsiding into that eerie twilit world in which perfect strangers might tell each other their most intimate secrets.

'Hi Sherrie. Soraya.'

Soraya turned to face her.

'Heard the latest?'

'What latest?'

'Someone's been leaking stories to the press. About Sven being – you know . . .'

'Gay, you mean?'

'No, not that. About him doing time in Walton for fraud. It's all over page three of the *Courier*. Marsha hit

STRANGERS IN THE NIGHT

the roof. Didn't you see the papers today?'

April smiled.

'I'm a creature of the night, remember? I spend all day hanging upside down in my cave.'

'What I can't understand is why anybody'd want to do a thing like that,' mused Sherrie, throwing a silk scarf round her neck. 'Sven's such a pussycat.'

'And how many people know about Sven's past anyway?' pointed out Soraya. 'It has to be someone from the station.'

'But that's crazy,' protested Sherrie. 'Who'd want to badmouth the station they work for? It's crazy. Things are insecure enough already, what with the franchise being up for renewal in a few months' time.'

April took the stairs down to the basement, where a suite of new studios had recently been installed. Even brand new equipment and two coats of magnolia emulsion did little to dispel the gloom or the fusty atmosphere of the old custom house, but April felt comfortable down here. She'd got to know her studio well over the weeks she'd been doing the night time show. It was beginning to feel like home.

The clock ticked slowly round towards midnight. The witching hour. The time when unusual people picked up the 'phone and dialled up 'Strangers in the Night'.

April thought fleetingly of Sven Harlesson. Bad luck that, Sven was an OK sort of guy. Weird business too. As weird as Marsha Fox, smiling at her over the lunch table and telling her 'not to let "Strangers in the Night" become too successful.' Just what, exactly, was going on at Mersey Roar?

41

Aurelia Clifford

And what did Marsha Fox know that she wasn't telling?

She was sliding cartridges into the tape machine and checking the 'phone lines when a shadow fell across the desk. Odd that. Sherrie and Soraya had gone, and the building was to all intents and purposes empty.

Turning round, she saw the silhouette of a man standing in the corridor outside the studio. A man with a long overcoat and a hat pulled down low. She couldn't make out his face. What the hell was he doing here, now, at this time of the night . . .? He seemed to be staring through the glass. Staring straight at her as though he was trying to read the secrets of her soul.

The clock registered eight minutes to midnight. She had a show to present. There was no time for any of this. But April got to her feet and walked towards the studio door, determined to find out what was going on.

'Hey – you, what do you think you're doing? You're not supposed to be in here.'

Before she was out of the studio the man was up and running, disappearing down the corridor into the maze of tunnels which led underneath the Victorian building. On impulse she gave chase, following the sound of his footsteps on the old tiled floor.

'Stop. Stop, I want to talk to you.'

It was useless. Her high heeled shoes prevented her running fast enough to catch him, and he seemed to know the labyrinth of corridors even better than she did. Maybe it was something and nothing. And in any case, what good would it do to be afraid? Besides, she had a date with a thousand invisible lovers.

STRANGERS IN THE NIGHT

Walking back towards her studio, April noticed that there was a light on in one of the neighbouring studios. Strange. No one else should be down here, no one else but Mike Meen was broadcasting tonight, and he used one of the first floor studios. Maybe the intruder had got in and stolen something . . . Maybe he'd doubled back and was in there even now.

As she approached the studio and looked through the window, she saw that Kieran Harte was inside. But he wasn't alone. He was laughing and joking with a red haired girl in the skimpiest of little black dresses. Her full breasts jiggled as she shook her hair back over her shoulders and stepped up to the microphone.

'OK, Asia,' she heard Kieran say. 'Counting you in now, two, three, four . . .'

The girl was singing new jingles for Kieran's show, the same words over and over again. 'Kieran Harte, the only start, to your perfect day . . .'

April had meant to walk straight in but instead she stood, frozen, outside the door. What was this icy feeling in the pit of her stomach – jealousy? No, that was too absurd. Why would she feel jealous of Kieran Harte and his bimbo chanteuse? That girl's breasts were ridiculously large, her hair was obviously dyed and, let's face it, she didn't even have a very good voice.

It came as quite a shock to realise that she was behaving like a spurned lover. She knew she ought simply to turn round and walk away, back to her studio and her programme and the 'phone lines that pleaded to be answered. But she couldn't take her eyes off Kieran. The way he

43

looked at that girl. The way she smiled back at him and bent low over him so that his eyes were on a level with the fullness of her cleavage. The way his hand slipped so naturally down the slope of her back as she bent over the console, hanging on every word he spoke.

How could I possibly want you, Kieran Harte? Want you to do that to me? Beg you to put your hands on my backside and push up my skirt and . . .? Don't flatter yourself, Kieran. I wouldn't want you if you were the last man on earth.

He looked up at that moment, saw April standing outside the studio door and waved in her direction.

'Come in.'

She shook her head.

'Come IN.'

Reluctantly she pushed open the door.

'Hi April, this is Asia, we're working together.'

'Is that what they're calling it these days?'

Kieran chose to ignore the jibe.

'What do you reckon to the new jingle?'

'Corny, dated and utterly unmemorable.'

'I knew you'd love it.'

Asia spat a ball of chewing gum into a paper handkerchief and threw it into the bin. What a slut, thought April. And probably twice as thick as her Liverpool accent.

'Who's the bitch?' enquired the girl with minimal interest.

'Asia Starr, meet April Sanchez.'

A slow smile spread over Asia's face.

STRANGERS IN THE NIGHT

'Yeah? April Sanchez, off "Strangers in the Night"? I've heard about your show, my Dad says it's pornographic.'

'I'm surprised he can pronounce it,' muttered April under her breath.

'*What*?'

'So what are you doing here then, Kieran?' enquired April. 'Aren't you missing out on your beauty sleep?'

'I'm gorgeous enough already. Besides, Asia's only available for singing work in the evenings. She's a barmaid in the daytime.' He exchanged a look with her that said, 'and later on she'll be sharing my bed.'

'Can I have a word with you, Kieran? Outside.'

'Yeah. I suppose so.' Puzzled, Kieran got up and followed April out into the corridor. 'What's all this then? Shouldn't you be presenting your show?'

'Yeah. In a minute.' She checked the clock. Only a couple of minutes to go. 'I've just seen some stranger wandering around the station.'

'Nah. That'll be Mike Meen, they don't come much stranger than him.'

'I'm serious, Kieran. There's an intruder. He was watching me.'

She saw that Kieran was about to say something flippant, then changed his mind at the last moment. When his hand stroked the back of her hair she didn't push him away, though Asia Starr was glaring at her through the studio window. To her surprise, she realised that she was shaking.

'What happened?'

45

Aurelia Clifford

'He was staring through my studio window. I tried running after him but he got away. He seemed to know the place, he could be anywhere by now . . .'

'It's OK, April. You go back to your studio and take care of the show. I'll take a look round, see if he's still here.' Kieran touched her face and as she looked up into his face she found herself wishing that he would kiss her. 'You do trust me, don't you?'

She wanted to tell him yes, because for once he was saying all the right things and his touch felt insanely good; but how could she? How could she ever be completely sure?

'This is April Sanchez, calling all Strangers in the Night. Call me, you know it's good to talk . . .'

She faded up the music.

'And after this, the big interview.'

Dan Lauren came up behind her and slipped his arms about her waist. His face nuzzled into the nape of her neck, the very tip of his tongue lightly brushing the tiny hairs and making them erect.

'Dan . . . you shouldn't!'

'Who's to see? You said yourself, we're completely alone.' Dan's hands slid down April's flanks, exploring the delicate combination of softness and hardness beneath her clothes. 'You look great in this dress, April. Correction, you *feel* great.'

It was modest by April's standards, a sleeveless sheath dress of plain red leather, smooth and closecut. A zipper extended down the front of the dress, from neckline to

STRANGERS IN THE NIGHT

hem, and Dan amused himself by toying with the tag, which was decorated with two red silk tassels. He eased it down a couple of inches, revealing a hint of black lace underwear. April laughed and pushed his hand away, pulling the zipper back up. She spun round to face Dan, wagging her finger at him.

'Naughty, naughty. Bad boy.'

He caught her fingers and kissed them, each in turn.

'You know you wouldn't want me any other way.'

'Maybe. Maybe not.' Tonight she felt hyped-up and sexy, a crimson leather vamp with black shiny fingernails and underwear that heightened her arousal with every moment she made. 'But you promised you'd behave yourself, remember? The interview's coming up after this record.'

'Reluctantly Dan sat down in a chair opposite April.

'What do you want me to talk about?'

'Anything you like.'

'*Anything*? You mean that?'

'The sexier the better. They want to hear everything. Tell them what it's like to own a record company, what it was like to be in a successful band.' Her eyes met Dan's. 'Tell them your fantasies.'

The record ended and April nodded to Dan.

'Ready?'

Dan leaned forward and laid his hand on her stockinged knee.

'Ready for anything.'

'April Sanchez calling all you night owls and moon children. Tonight I have Dan Lauren with me, chief

47

executive of Viper Sounds and former lead singer with indie band Outside My Shadow. Dan, it's great to talk to you.'

'Great to be here, April.' The hand pushed April's skirt just a fraction higher, exposing an extra inch or so of shapely leg. 'A real pleasure.'

'Are you a night owl, Dan? Or an early bird?'

'I love the night. That's when I have all my most . . . creative thoughts. And I feel more alive at night. More sexually charged.'

'So tell me, Dan. You started your music career with Liverpool band Outside My Shadow, and had a lot of success in the UK charts but you never quite made it big in the States. Why was that?'

Dan smiled and drew his chair closer to April's, so that his knee slid between hers.

'I guess that would be because of the sex scandal.'

'Yeah? Why don't you tell us all about that, Dan?' Her voice was husky and sweet. It never wavered, not even when Dan placed his two hands on her legs and started sliding them up underneath the skirt of her dress.

'We were touring the Mid West. It was one night in Oklahoma – Godawful craphole of a place. We'd been doing a gig at some city hall and, yeah, we were mellow, we'd dropped a little acid . . .'

'So what happened, Dan?'

'We met a few girls, took them back to our hotel.' Dan's fingers were climbing April's dress, sliding up over the swell of her breasts to the tasselled zipper. 'There was one . . . she was blonde, sixteen or maybe seventeen. She

STRANGERS IN THE NIGHT

had the most incredible body, like a kind of teenage Marilyn Monroe, you know? Rounded and full, but with a tiny waist and these long, long legs.'

'Do you remember her name?'

'As a matter of fact I do. It was Mary Jo. Mary Jo Darnell. She had candy pink lipstick and blue glitter eyeshadow, and she was wearing this incredibly tight red dress.'

Dan had the tag of the zipper in his hand. He drew it down so slowly and carefully that it made only the softest whispering sound as it crept downwards, revealing the black lace basque beneath the red leather dress.

April could scarcely breathe for the wicked excitement of the moment. So what if they were alone at the radio station? So what if no one could possibly find them out? In her mind's eye she could picture the eyes of a thousand listeners, watching in the darkness, glittering in the shadows. She could almost hear their breathing quicken as they saw Dan stripping the dress from her shoulders, revealing the opalescent whiteness of her breasts, nestling in a frill of jet black lace. It was an effort to say anything at all.

'You . . . made out . . . with Mary Jo?'

Dan chuckled. His hands roamed over April's breasts, stroking them as though they were frightened pet animals, coaxing and caressing the nipples into hardness as he gently rubbed them through the cups of the basque.

'We were in the lift at the hotel, me and Mary Jo and Mary Jo's friend Jaime. Now Jaime wasn't my type if you know what I mean, too skinny and too worldlywise. In

49

those days I liked my groupies young and impressionable. Jaime'd been everywhere, seen everything, screwed everything. She told me she had this friend who went round rock stars with Cynthia Plastercaster, having sex with them and taking plaster casts of their dicks. Can you believe that?'

He slipped his hands into the cups of April's basque, scooping her breasts into his palms and drawing them out, resting them on the underwiring so that they thrust forwards and upwards, shamelessly aggressive in their demands. April could hardly bear to look at them. They were painfully sensitive, and seemed to be silently screaming 'Suck us, bite us, squeeze us together and fuck us.'

'So you ditched Jaime?'

'Uh-oh.'

'But you said . . .'

'I most probably *would have* ditched her, only the lift broke down, it got stuck between the thirtieth and the thirty first floors. And there I was, stuck with the two of them. Not that I was ungrateful, you don't look a gift horse in the mouth. Hey, and what a mouth she had . . .'

Dan was massaging April's breasts now, squeezing and kneading them whilst his knee pushed further and deeper into the valley between her parted thighs. Her black panties were soaked through with the sweet elixir of her arousal. She wanted to warn him to stop . . . and to beg him to go on and on and on.

'She was good?'

'The best . . . almost.' Those dark eyes were making their meaning very clear. The best, April. Except for you.

STRANGERS IN THE NIGHT

'She gave me head while I was warming up Mary Jo, she was kind of nervous. Turned out later it was only her second time. Incredible body she had, really soft but firm too and with this skin like Limoges porcelain.

'I had her standing up, with her legs wrapped round my waist and all the time Jaime's licking and biting my backside. It was pretty wild, even now it excites me when I think about it. Anyhow, that's how they found us when they opened up the lift to get us out.'

'They?'

'The county fire service. It might have helped if I'd known Mary Jo's father was the local Fire Chief . . . They ran us out of town for "corrupting minors" and we never really got off the ground in the US after that. We were big in Germany and Japan though.'

Dan put his hands on April's waist and pulled her to her feet. She knew what he meant to do. She shook her head. He smiled and nodded emphatically, then let his hand drop to the base of her belly. The first touch of his fingers on the pouting flesh of her labia made her stumble and gasp, unable to speak for several seconds. With an effort she recovered her composure.

'S-so. Dan. Perhaps you could tell us about life as a record producer?'

The fingers intensified their torment, probing a little deeper into the slippery satin groove formed as her wet pants worked their way between the outer lips of her sex.

'I'd be delighted, April. Whatever you want. Just say the word.'

The glancing contact of his finger on her clitoris was

too much to bear. Colour burned on April's cheeks, she pushed him away and made a grab for the control panel.

'I'll be back with Dan Lauren after this record.' The music crashed in, loud and stormy, last year's winners of the Mersey Roar 'Battle of the Bands', and Dan's newest signing.

'Better make that two records. No, three.' Dan slotted two more CDs into the machine.

'Dan, no. We can't! Not here.'

'Who's to see?' He unzipped his flies and took out his swollen shaft, cradling it in his palm, offering it to her. The ring that pierced its tip glinted in the low studio lighting. 'We fucked in the street. On that building site, don't you remember?'

'That's not the point, we . . .'

Dan had hold of her and was pulling down her panties, forcing them down to her knees then letting gravity do the rest.

'Don't fight me, April, it makes no sense. You want this every bit as much as I do.'

'No!'

'Yes.'

He stopped her protests with a kiss, sliding his hands underneath her buttocks and lifting her up. He was every bit as strong as he looked, thought April through the mist of angry lust. A daily session at the gym had kept his body supple, powerful, exquisitely muscled.

Still kissing her, he lifted her until she was above his waist. She had given up fighting now, all she wanted was to surrender to the warm seductive glow of this new and

STRANGERS IN THE NIGHT

exciting game. Instinctively she wrapped her legs around Dan's waist. His skin felt hot and slightly sticky through his white silk shirt, with the hardness of tensed muscle close beneath.

Dan responded by releasing her from his predatory kiss. She emerged gasping, breathless, her head spinning.

'This is crazy, Dan. *You're* crazy.'

'Taking what you want is never crazy.'

He lowered her in a single, sudden movement onto the upraised spike of his penis. She tried not to make a sound, but the pleasure was too violent and she let out a shuddering, moaning sigh. In any case, what did it matter? Why not abandon herself to what she felt, take what she wanted and tell the world to go to hell?

She thought fleetingly of the intruder she had almost caught three nights ago; and of Kieran Harte, who tended to turn up unannounced in the most inconvenient places. Like here and now, in her thoughts, when they should be filled with her lust for Daniel Lauren.

But Kieran would not intrude on them tonight. Tonight she and Dan were alone, with no one to spy on them but silent strangers and the dark, velvety, unquestioning night.

Chapter 4

'This is Mike Meen on Mersey Roar, taking you into the warzone with "Battle of the Bands" . . .'

April wriggled on her seat in the too hot, too cramped first floor studio. It was also far too small to accommodate Mike and his sound gear, the 'celebrity' judges and tonight's contestants, three young local bands with their eyes on the 'Battle of the Bands' final at the Philharmonic Hall, a cheque for three thousand pounds and a recording contract with the competition's sponsors, Viper Sounds.

Tonight's heat featured Casbah Swing, a four piece acid jazz outfit from Allerton; Wirral's heavy metal mobsters, Axehead; and Taradiddle, who played nice tunes your mum would like and hadn't got a hope in Hell.

'Great legs, April,' observed a voice at her side. It was her co-judge, ex-punk rocker turned sculptor, Dip Theria. Looking down, April noticed that the distance between his thigh and hers was small and decreasing. 'I like a woman who keeps herself in shape. You wouldn't fancy modelling for me, I don't suppose?'

'Thanks but no thanks, Dip.' She thought of his latest

55

Aurelia Clifford

'masterpiece', a pickled buffalo with an inflatable naked woman riding on its back. It had won him the Turner Prize and a death threat from the Animal Liberation Front. 'Formaldehyde brings me out in a rash.'

'I was thinking more of painting you with melted chocolate and charging punters to lick it off. Course, I'd have to shave off all your body hair first . . .'

Dip was making no secret of rubbing up against her, his denimed thigh sliding over her shiny black PVC pants. She made a point of moving her chair a couple of inches further away, but he simply slid after her.

'I've just bought a penthouse overlooking the Albert Dock.'

'Yeah?' April hoped her disinterest would put him off.

'Sixth floor, great view.' Thigh slid against thigh, with a sound like the swish of wet raincoats in a backstreet cinema. 'Ever made love on a waterbed, have you?'

'Can't say I have.' She flashed Dip a smile. 'I get seasick.'

'So we'll do it on a rug on the floor. You and I could be good together, April. I could be great for your image.'

In desperation, April walked across the studio and tapped Mike Meen on the shoulder. He finished briefing the lead singer from Axehead, put on a record and turned round.

'Thanks for coming, April. Good of you to step in at the last minute.'

'Pleasure.' She nodded towards Dip Theria. 'But you might have warned me about him.'

Mike sniggered.

'Been chatting you up, has he?'

STRANGERS IN THE NIGHT

'I wouldn't say it was anything that subtle. He's the bloody human octopus.'

'And filthy rich with it. OK, so he's nothing to write home about, but he has possibilities – and you could keep your eyes closed.'

'Come off it, Mike.' She looked him up and down, not exactly Mister Dangerous in his cuddly sleeveless sweater and cord pants. 'I'd rather sleep with you, and that's saying something.'

Mike grinned.

'I'll bear it in mind. Now you know what to do, don't you? Marsha's briefed you?'

'Yeah, yeah. Be honest but not too honest. Don't hurt anybody's feelings.'

'They're all great bands. With the right management, Axehead could be the next Sepultura.'

April cast an eye over Axehead, who were tuning up ready for their first song. She'd always had a bit of a thing about heavy metal bands, with their hard, pulsating rhythms and screaming guitars, but there wasn't much to tempt her appetite for them tonight. This lot looked like fifth formers with shaggy perms and leopardskin pants sprayed onto tight little backsides. All very nice if you were a sixteen year old virgin, but April had left that phase behind a long time ago. And after you'd had Daniel Lauren, it wasn't easy to imagine ever wanting another man. Unless that man might be . . .

She pushed the thought out of her mind as Mike started waxing lyrical about some other discovery he'd just made.

'Hmm? What's that . . .?'

'VanillaSex, April. I was just telling you about them. They're fantastic, won the last heat . . .'

She shrugged.

'Can't say I've ever heard of them.'

Mike smiled.

'You will, mark my words. VanillaSex are going all the way.'

Dip Theria sidled up and slid his hand into the back pocket of April's PVC jeans.

'Ready to go, babe?' He reinforced the double entendre with a quick pinch of April's backside. She responded by accidentally elbowing him in the stomach, setting off a coughing fit.

Axehead were not the next Sepultura, not even the next Barron Knights. If you were feeling charitable you might call them dull. Dip Theria obviously loved them, but then what did he know? April chewed the end of her pen and winced at another off-key guitar break. It was going to be difficult to find anything good to say about this one . . .

'Where are we going?'

'I'm taking you out for lunch.'

'But where?'

'You'll see. A little place in the country I happen to know.' Dan handed April a black motorcycle helmet with a dark, tinted visor. 'Why don't you get on and find out where?'

Dan Lauren's Harley Davidson was parked in the underground car park of his exclusive apartment block.

STRANGERS IN THE NIGHT

Even in the semi-darkness it gleamed, a perfect creation of black chassis and polished chrome.

April slid her leg over the seat and found the footrest. The leather upholstery was springy and cold between her thighs. She switched on the tiny microphone in the helmet.

'You should have told me we were going by bike, I would have worn trousers.'

'That's precisely why I didn't tell you.' He mounted the bike, kicking away the side stand, and she saw him looking at her in the rearview mirror.

'Like what you see?' she enquired.

He reached round behind him and ran his leather-gauntleted hand up her bare thigh.

'Do you really need to ask?'

'We could skip lunch. Go to bed.'

'Trust me, April. The waiting will be worth it.'

Jabbing the ignition, Dan eased the Harley up the slope towards the street level. At first the bright spring sunlight blinded April and she pushed down her visor, grateful for the anonymity it offered. Her arms were round Dan's waist as he squeezed open the throttle and the bike leapt forward.

It was a warm day but once out of the centre of town they were doing sixty five and the wind felt cold on April's bare legs and arms. She felt incredibly visible on the Harley, her short skirt high on her thighs and her knees pressed tight against Dan's flanks. People stopped to stare, their eyes following the bike, gazing at the girl with the short, short skirt and the long bare legs, her breasts pressed up against the back of her lover's leather jacket, her hands curled round his waist.

'People are staring at me, Dan.'

She heard him laugh, the sound peculiarly electronic as it came through on the headset.

'You love it, April. You love it when people stare at your body. You know damn well they're lusting after you.'

She laid her face against his back and whispered to him over the noise of the engine.

'Does it make you jealous, Dan?'

Dan's gloved right hand stroked April's bare thigh.

'I've always found jealousy the ultimate erotic stimulus, haven't you?'

'They're looking at me. They want my body. They want to screw me.'

'And I want to watch. I want to watch you getting it on with all these strangers. Every night on your show you lead them on. What if they all turned up at the studio one night, what if they all wanted your body?'

A picture formed in April's mind. A picture of faces pressed up against the glass panel of the studio window. Faces, faces, dozens of them, contorted with lust, mouthing soundless obscenities. Hands clawing at the glass, pulling at clothes, baring the pink sticky wetness of swollen dicks that left opaque smears and trickles on the glass. She tried to focus on the mouths, opening and closing, the lips forming themselves into words.

'Fuck, fuck, fuck. We want to fuck you, April. We're going to take you.'

Afraid, aroused, ashamed of that arousal, she tried to

STRANGERS IN THE NIGHT

chase the images from her head. They were speeding along a Cheshire lane now, hedges and trees and fields blurring into uniform green. The wind was buffeting April's arms and legs, catching the hem of her skirt and lifting it even higher.

'Is that what turns you on, Dan? The thought of watching me having sex with someone else?'

'It turns you on too. It's no use denying it.'

No. No use at all. April's body was warm and tense with the memory of the thought. For a few short moments she had lived the images in her mind, and she had welcomed those faceless lovers, hungry for their anonymous sex.

The broad seat of the Harley Davidson was hot now, warmed by the friction of her sex and thighs as they slid softly back and forth over the polished leather. She had to spread her legs very wide to ride the Harley, and her sex was gaping open beneath the thin film of her cotton briefs. Excited by the sensation, she slipped her hands a little lower and began to stroke Dan through his leathers. He was beautifully hard, his dick upright and swollen, tantalising her with what she wanted but could not have. Not yet . . .

The pillion seat was shaped slightly at the front, forming a low, hard ridge between her and Dan. As the bike bumped over ruts and loose stones, she was jolted forward and her wide open sex jarred against it, sending shocks through her whole body. She tried bracing herself against the movements of the bike, but there was pleasure in the discomfort, and she quickly found herself anticipating the next jolt, forcing herself a fraction further forward so that

61

her clitoris was stimulated for just a little longer. Much more, much more of this pleasurable torment, and she would blossom into secret, silent ecstasy.

'Does it feel good, April?'

'Good. Yes, good . . .'

Hand on the throttle, keeping it open, Dan reached round and touched April's belly. She slid a little further back, letting him in, knowing by instinct what he would do. She was not disappointed. His fingers slipped down to the swell of her pubis, rubbing it hard through her skirt.

'I can make it feel even better.'

'Oh. No, Dan, I can't bear it, I can't . . . oh!'

He made her come with a kind of cold efficiency which was paradoxically very, very arousing. It was like being masturbated by a beautiful robot, a wonderful automaton in warm and fragrant leather. In seconds his fingers took her to the edge and drove her over the precipice.

The pleasure was dangerous and very, very potent. It left her dizzy and disorientated, clinging blindly to Dan, suddenly terrified of the speed and the noise and the flickering patterns of sunlight and leaves. Where was she, who was she, what were these incredible feelings that shook her like a rag doll and left her weak and helpless?

She raised her head as she felt the Harley move down through the gears, slow down and coast to a halt.

'Where are we?' She lifted her visor and eased the helmet off, shaking out her hair.

Dan got off the bike, lifting it onto its stand. They

STRANGERS IN THE NIGHT

were parked by the front steps of a large country house, probably eighteenth century. A woman in a short white uniform dress was walking down the steps towards them.

'Ragwell Hall.' Dan took off his helmet and put it into the topbox at the back of the Harley.

'Ragwell . . . isn't that some kind of health farm?'

Dan met her horrified gaze with laughter.

'Sure is.'

'You said you were taking me out for lunch! Have I given up my afternoon off for half a sprout and a glass of carrot juice?'

'Let's just say I think you'll be pleasantly surprised.'

The woman in the white dress was smiling as though she'd just bumped into a long lost friend.

'Mr Lauren, how lovely to see you again. And this must be Ms Sanchez?'

Dan held out his hand.

'Samantha, long time no see. Is everything ready?'

'Exactly as you requested, Mr Lauren. If you and Ms Sanchez would like to follow me, I've had the Grantchester Suite prepared especially for you.'

Mystified, April followed Samantha along the corridor. It didn't *look* like a health farm. For a start off there were no sweating bodies in tracksuits, and there wasn't a brussel sprout in sight. Still, appearances could be deceptive.

Samantha stopped in front of panelled double doors, painted eggshell white edged with matt gold. A brass plate announced 'Grantchester Suite'.

'I'll leave you two to . . . relax. Everything should be

Aurelia Clifford

exactly as you ordered it. Just ring the bell if you need anything else.'

The Grantchester Suite was certainly no ordinary hotel suite. April walked in stunned silence from room to room. Private gym, pool, dining table set with exotic fruits, olives, seafood canapes, double bedroom with mirrored ceiling and gauzy drapes . . .

'Dan – this is bigger than my entire flat!'

He swung round to face her, unzipped his bike jacket and dropped it onto a rather nice scroll end sofa.

'Hungry?'

Head on one side, she dragged the tangled hair back from her face.

'Not for food.'

'Not even oysters and fresh papaya?'

She stepped closer to Dan and, slipping her hands behind his head, drew his mouth down to hers. The kiss was long and intense.

'Later maybe.' She surveyed the luxury around her. It was hard to know where to start. 'Did you arrange all of this . . . for me?'

'Naturally.'

'Are you always this extravagant?'

'Only in matters of pleasure. Pleasure sharpens the mind, so few people really understand that. And in the music business it pays to stay sharp, April. There's always someone waiting for a chance to destroy you. The trick is to get in first.'

She looked at him, puzzled. There was no mistaking the hard edge in his voice.

STRANGERS IN THE NIGHT

'Is anything wrong?'

'Not now I've got you here alone.'

'I could get used to this kind of luxury.'

'That . . . could be arranged.'

She looked at him, intrigued.

'What are you saying?'

He shrugged.

'Only that I have what it takes to make you happy and keep you that way. Remember that the next time you let some creep get close to you.'

'W-what do you mean?'

'I mean, April, remember all the things I can give you the next time Kieran Harte tries to move in on you.'

'Kieran? Kieran Harte?' April stared in amazement at Dan. 'You're not jealous of Kieran, you can't be!'

'The question is, have I any reason to be?'

Dan's question stunned April for a moment. It was several telling seconds before she was able to laugh and tell him:

'There's no man I want but you, Dan. How could Kieran Harte ever compete with you?'

OK April Sanchez, said a quiet voice in her head. Prove it. Prove that it's Dan you want, prove that you don't feel anything when Kieran's hand touches yours and you find yourself gazing into those deep blue eyes.

'Come with me, Dan.' She took him by the hand.

'What is this?'

'Come into here.' She led Dan towards the bed. 'I'm going to show you how much I want you. And I'm going to make you feel better than you've ever felt before.'

65

Aurelia Clifford

★ ★ ★

They didn't make it to the bed.

Before they were halfway across the room, they were rolling and tumbling over and over on the Chinese silk carpet, and April was ripping off Dan's shirt, unbuckling his trousers, stripping and clawing at his gloriously golden flesh.

In a matter of moments her panties were a screwed up ball of cotton on the floor and she was straddling him, her thighs tight about his torso, imprisoning him in the cage of her lust. He was gazing up at her, a delighted half smile on his lips.

'You little vixen.'

'You're mine now, Dan.'

'So what are you going to do with me?'

'Easy. I'm going to drive you crazy.'

His manhood was between her thighs. Pushing down, she trapped it between the long, slippery groove of her sex and the flat muscle of his belly. Tilting her pelvis she drew herself back and forth, pressing down on his dick, anointing it with smooth sweetness as she reached backwards between her legs and stroked and squeezed his balls. She was in control now, not Dan. She was the one calling the shots, setting the rhythm, pushing him to the very edge of pleasure and then refusing him the final release.

'Want me, Dan?'

'I'd have thought that was obvious.'

'You'll have to do better than that.'

Dan's hands were on April's buttocks, his fingers

STRANGERS IN THE NIGHT

clutching handfuls of flesh, trying to make her do it the way he wanted. But she resisted him.

'April, I want you now.'

'When I'm ready. First, you're going to give me what I want.'

She slid up his body, her sex skimming his belly and chest, smearing them with her moisture. She used it to draw circles on his flesh, spirals and intricate patterns; magical symbols of this new and exhilarating possession.

He did not make a sound as she lowered her sex onto his face, cradling his head, holding it firm for her to grind her pleasure from nose and mouth and tongue. She felt his lips part and he began biting and licking the sensitive frills of flesh, making her dance on his face, swivelling and tilting her hips, swaying and moaning and all the time pleasuring herself with Dan's head between her legs.

April's earlier orgasm had made her clitoris extra sensitive. She could hardly bear the roughness of Dan's unshaven stubble, or the wicked nips of his teeth as he alternated sucking and licking with biting. Was this pleasure or discomfort? It was so difficult to tell. But one thing was for certain: it was taking over her body, making her feel light as a cork bobbing on a boiling sea.

Dan's fingers were rebellious. They knew with all the wickedness in them that it would take hardly anything, almost nothing, to bring her excitement to a crescendo. They began innocently enough, gently tickling her buttocks, teasing the tiny hairs with the very lightest of touches. But their caresses became bolder, and moments later April felt Dan's fingers sliding into the deep crease between her arse cheeks.

Automatically she tensed every muscle against him, but Dan knew what she wanted before she realised it herself. Her secret rose blossomed instantly as his index finger plunged into the depths of her anus, penetrating her like the second dick she craved.

'Yes. Yes, Dan. Yes, yes, YES!'

She would punish him for this, she decided as she gave herself up to the pleasure and her juices cascaded onto Dan's upturned face. She would tease him until he screamed for mercy, and then she would screw him quickly and savagely, sucking every drop of semen out of him.

No doubt tomorrow she would allow herself to be Dan Lauren's plaything again. But here and now, for a few delicious hours, she intended to enjoy her sensual power to the full.

The warm, lazy glow of physical satisfaction couldn't last long. There was a show to plan, live interviews to set up . . . and there was Marsha Fox.

April got the message late that afternoon, when she called in at the station to catch up on some work. Sherrie called her over as she was walking through reception.

'Message for you, April. From Marsha.' She handed over several folded scraps of paper. 'Three actually. She's been calling you all day, here and at home.'

'It's my afternoon off, for pity's sake. It's about time Marsha Fox stopped thinking she owns me twenty four hours a day.'

STRANGERS IN THE NIGHT

'Whatever. Anyhow, it looks urgent. She's in her office if you want to go straight up and see her.'

Frankly, April would rather have put her head in a tiger's mouth, but seeing as that option wasn't on offer she took the lift to the fourth floor. The door to Marsha Fox's office stood slightly ajar, and April caught snatches of a bad tempered conversation.

'. . . just *do* it. Look, it's not down to me, I don't make the policy around here . . . Do it or get out . . . is that simple enough for you to understand?'

April hesitated. Would anyone but a fool go in there at this precise moment? But then again, Marsha Fox was never what you'd call mellow. She knocked on the door and heard the sound of the telephone receiver being slammed onto the hook.

'Not now, I'm busy.'

April pushed the door a little further open.

'I heard it was urgent.'

Marsha threw down her pen and sat back in her chair.

'Oh. You.'

'So, do I come in or go away?'

'Come in, shut the door and shut up.'

'What am I supposed to have done this time?' April refused the offer of a chair and Marsha got to her feet so that the two women were eye to eye across the desk.

'I thought you'd learned your lesson, April. Obviously you're stupider than I'd thought.'

'What's this all about?'

Marsha walked across to the filing cabinet, took out a sheaf of papers and slapped them down on the desk.

'Recognise this, April?'

April glanced down at the desk.

'What about it?'

'It's the playlist, April. The approved playlist for your show. Or has that small fact escaped your notice?'

'It's crap. Nobody wants to listen to that MOR rubbish, not even in the middle of the night. With better music I'll get higher listening figures, it stands to reason. I thought . . .

'You're not paid to think,' snapped Marsha.

'So it would seem.'

Marsha thumped down her fist on the desk. Her pen rolled to edge and fell off onto the carpet.

'Listen carefully, April. This is the approved playlist and you will stick to it, do you understand?'

'But *why*? I don't understand . . .'

'There are a lot of things you don't understand. Things you don't *want* to understand, believe me.'

Marsha's lips were trembling, very wet and glossy with spittle. All of a sudden April noticed that they were red as ripe fruit, biteable and succulent.

'Look, Marsha, I'm sorry if I'm causing trouble for you, but you're telling me to compromise my standards . . .'

Marsha laughed, but there was no humour in the sound. To April's astonishment she seized her hands, forcing her to look into her dark brown eyes.

'Standards, April? Is that what you think this is all about? Listen to me, standards are the least of this station's problems and if you have any sense you'll realise that.'

STRANGERS IN THE NIGHT

'But Marsha, I . . .'

'There are people who want to protect you, April. Do exactly as you're told and you'll be all right.'

'Protect me – from what?'

'Will you *listen* to me? They want to protect you, but if you won't help yourself, what can they do?'

April understood nothing of what Marsha was saying; but there was no mistaking the look in her eyes. She had never seen Marsha Fox show fear before. And there was more to it than that, another emotion, something darker and more menacing than fear. April found herself responding to it in spite of herself. It seemed to soak into her through her skin, filling her with a kind of guilty warmth she scarcely dared acknowledge.

Her lips were very close to Marsha's, a matter of a few inches, no more. It would have been so very easy to lean a little closer and press her mouth against Marsha's, to taste the warmth of those moist lips . . .

Perhaps she would have done, perhaps not. At that moment the door opened and April heard a familiar voice blurt out a few embarrassed words. Jerking her hands out of Marsha's, she turned to see Kieran Harte standing on the threshold, not quite sure whether or not he ought to turn and walk away.

'April . . . Marsha.' He swallowed. 'I'm not interrupting anything, am I?'

That night the show went even better than usual – well enough for April to put all the nagging worries out of her mind, for a few hours at least. What was going on with

Marsha Fox? What was she going to say to Kieran Harte when she next saw him? To hell with it, it would all have sorted itself out by tomorrow.

She played a record while she lined up callers. Phil from Greasby was back; there seemed to be no getting rid of him.

'Look Phil, for the last time, Aleister Crowley did *not* discover the Beatles.'

'But April, if you take *Sergeant Pepper* and play it backwards . . .'

'One more word and I'm barring you, Phil, got that?'

'Yeah. Yeah, sorry. April . . .'

'What, Phil?'

'I love you, April, you're incredible, once you're really mine I'm going to . . .'

'Thank you, Phil, and goodnight.'

Phil gave up and rang off. Not that it would stop him ringing the show again, to tell her that the ancient Romans had invented custard or that everybody from Wigan is an extra terrestrial. There was no way to stop any of them talking, not now she'd got them to open up to her. Everyone wanted to talk to April Sanchez, to tell her something, nothing, anything, but just to keep on talking.

She glanced at the timer on the CD player. Only two and a half minutes to go before the next talk slot, and she didn't have anyone suitable yet. Wasn't there anyone with a secret fantasy, a sensual obsession, a message for a forbidden lover?

'OK, caller line 4. You're through to "Strangers in the Night". What would you like to talk about?'

STRANGERS IN THE NIGHT

After a pause a man's voice answered. It was deep and distorted, rather muffled.

'I've got a special message for you, April. Over your shoulder. Look over your shoulder.'

The line clicked dead.

Over her shoulder? What was that supposed to mean? She glanced right. Nothing. Then left – and then she saw it, a small shiny envelope pinned to the cork soundproofing tiles just behind her head. Her name was printed on it, in tall, anonymous letters.

She took it down, opened it, and slid out a photograph of Sven Harlesson. It was a prison mugshot: HMP Walton, Prisoner No RJ340328. Across it was scrawled, in bright red crayon:

IT COULD BE YOU.

At that moment the studio 'phone rang again and she answered it in a daze.

'Y-yes?'

'If you want to know more, April, play a record for me. Play *Every Breath You Take*, by the Police. You know the lyrics to that one, don't you? "Every breath you take . . . I'll be watching you."'

'Go ahead, April, why don't you play it? It's on the desk right in front of you.'

Chapter 5

April Sanchez waited. And then she waited some more. The photograph and cryptic message she had found in the studio could only be the start, of that she was certain – but the start of what?

Maybe it was a sick practical joke, someone at the station trying to unsettle her, make her lose concentration and foul up big time? But why? If that was true it made little sense, not when they were all supposed to be working towards the same goal: survival.

If someone at the station *was* behind all this, they weren't giving anything away. Could it be Sven? Hardly, he'd been in an impenetrable whisky delirium ever since that article in the *Courier*. Mike Meen? He didn't have the balls. Soraya? It was a faint possibility. Or Kieran Harte for that matter, but despite her determination to think the worst of him, April had to concede that this wasn't his style.

If she wanted to really use her imagination she could try and pin it all on Marsha Fox, with her gourmet taste in cruelty. After all, it was Marsha who had moved her from

75

the breakfast show, Marsha who'd found fault with everything she'd done and talked in riddles about trying to 'protect' her.

Protect her from what, that was the question.

April was on edge, but then so was everyone else. They all knew that Mersey Roar might soon stop existing – and then what? She'd heard a rumour that one or two DJs had started sounding out rival stations, trying to line up something to go to if the worst happened. That was probably the sensible thing to do, but right now April Sanchez had just two things on her mind: finding out who was trying to frighten her, and keeping 'Strangers in the Night' firmly on the road. *Her* road – not Kieran's, not Marsha's, not anybody else's either.

It wasn't too difficult to find things to occupy her mind. 'Battle of the Bands' provided occasional amusement when she wasn't working on 'Strangers', and Dan Lauren was enough to take anyone's mind off their problems. She'd mentioned the photo to him, just in passing. He'd laughed and kissed her, holding her face between his hands. She'd shaken off Dan's caresses, offended by his laughter . . . or perhaps angry at herself for taking it all so seriously.

'You think it's funny, don't you – you're telling me I'm paranoid, is that it?'

Dan's voice was soothing, conciliatory.

'Not at all. Have you . . . mentioned this to the police?'

'Of course.'

'And what did they say?'

Dan had touched a raw nerve.

STRANGERS IN THE NIGHT

'That it was just a practical joke, and I should try to get things into perspective.'

Dan smiled and stroked his fingers down the sides of her face to her bare shoulders. Even in her indignation her body responded to him with automatic shudders of longing. Beneath her thin cocktail dress her breasts tensed in eager anticipation, the nipples straining upwards to claim elusive kisses.

'For what it's worth, April, I think you should be flattered.'

'*Flattered*? Are you serious?'

'I never say anything that I don't mean.' This time Dan slipped down the straps of her dress and it slithered down over her breasts, exposing them to his long-awaited caresses. 'You see, April.' He paused to take one nipple between his teeth and tease moans of protesting pleasure from his lover's lips. 'You see, only the very beautiful and the irresistibly sensual inspire such obsessive devotion.'

She stared at him, caught between the hot urgency coursing down through her belly and the need to ask and answer questions.

'Yes, but this isn't about devotion, is it? This is about some sicko making threats, trying to frighten me . . .'

Dan left off running his tongue around April's swollen areola and gently lowered her onto the bed, rolling over until he was half on top of her, pinning her half naked body to the Egyptian cotton sheets.

'I'm no psychologist, but just say frightening you makes him feel important. Perhaps he needs to feel he possesses a part of your soul to get . . . aroused. Of course . . .' He

Aurelia Clifford

pushed up the skirt of April's dress and ran his hand thoughtfully down her flank. His hand felt furnace hot on her skin as his fingers teased their way inside her panties and began exploring the mound of her sex. 'Of course, it might not be a *him* at all. It could be a woman.'

For a split second, April's mind filled with the image of Marsha Fox, leaning towards her over her desk, those plum red lips moist and quivering, those hands encasing hers, drawing her inexorably closer . . .

'That's stupid, Dan. Women don't . . . women just aren't like that.'

'Yeah, stupid. You're right, April, forget I spoke.' The fingers slipped just a little further down, their very tips penetrating the deep valley between April's swollen pussy lips. 'Better still, forget the whole thing. It was just some-body's idea of a bad joke. And besides, who could possibly harm you while you've got me to protect you?'

It was impossible not to feel safe with Dan's body on top of hers, his hands working her like some simple engine of pleasure. But at night, in the semi-darkness of the studio, when strangers' voices whispered their secrets over the airwaves, it was difficult not to let imagination take over.

It was about this time that the letters started arriving at her flat. No, not letters exactly, cards – white with coloured pictures on the front, like a child's birthday card. The first had a picture of the White Rabbit on the front, his watch chain attached to the front of his red and yellow check waistcoat and his pocket watch in his hand. The card was blank inside. After puzzling over it for a few

STRANGERS IN THE NIGHT

minutes, April slid it into her handbag. Maybe it would all make sense later.

The same thing happened the next day. The card was exactly the same, with no message, nothing to indicate where it had come from, not even a legible postmark.

It was no great surprise when another card arrived on the third day. She almost threw it away without even opening it, but something – maybe curiosity, maybe a premonition – made her tear open the envelope and pull out the card.

Same picture. Identical. Without expecting to find anything, she flicked open the card. This time there was a message, laser printed to look like copperplate handwriting:

TIME PASSES, APRIL.
BE CAREFUL YOU DON'T PASS WITH IT.

Time? What time? What did it all mean? April stared at the picture on the front of the card, remembering how she'd hated *Alice in Wonderland* as a child. How did the story go? Pubescent know-it-all meets talking bunny and has conversations about jam. Yeah. Right.

She looked a little closer and saw that the Tenniel illustration wasn't quite right. She wondered why she hadn't noticed before that the White Rabbit was carrying a digital stopwatch. The face carried nothing that made any particular sense, just a number: '98'. Ninety eight *what*?

An idea struck her, and she fetched out the small metal

Aurelia Clifford

attaché case she used as a briefcase. The first two cards were still in there, buried under a pile of press releases and an article on having sex over the Internet. She took her cards out and laid them on the table next to the most recent. They were identical in every respect, except for one. On the second card, the White Rabbit's watch read '99'; in the first, '100'.

One hundred, ninety nine, ninety eight . . . it didn't take a genius to guess what tomorrow's card would say. But why? Why count down from one hundred?

On a whim, she got up and walked across to the kitchen calendar, counting down the days. Sixty, thirty four, twenty one, fourteen, nine, seven . . .

Zero. Somewhere at the back of her mind April had anticipated the date even before she'd started counting down. Day Zero was September 15: the very last day of Mersey Roar's broadcasting licence.

Kieran put on the headset and listened in. Asia was good at this, no doubt about it. She'd been completely wasted as a barmaid and a nightclub hostess. With some careful management, Asia Starr was going to become the new voice of electronic sex.

'. . . Is that what you want me to do, sir? Take off my bra? Mummy will be so angry if she knows I've shown you my bare breasts . . .'

He'd had no trouble getting permission to use one of the Mersey Roar studios to help Asia record her latest 0891 tape; he just hadn't bothered asking. What Marsha Fox didn't know about wouldn't hurt her, and the way

STRANGERS IN THE NIGHT

things were going they'd all be out of a job in three or four months' time anyway. This was certainly more fun than demonstrating carpet cleaner in Woolworth's.

'. . . Oh sir, *sir*, you mustn't do that, whatever will Mummy say?'

The busty sixteen year old schoolgirl routine would be a wow with the punters. It was certainly having the desired effect on Kieran. He could hardly keep his hands from his dick as he sat back, closed his eyes and listened to Asia's voice floating round and round inside his head.

'. . . Nobody's ever touched me there . . . oh, it feels lovely! Will you do it again, sir? Shall I bend over this chair and let you pull down my knickers?'

Asia wasn't just good at *talking* about sex. She'd practically thrown herself at Kieran and he'd been brought up to believe that no gentleman should ever refuse a lady. Not that Asia was exactly that . . .

They'd had three or four all night sessions at Kieran's flat. With her white-blonde highlights and Pamela Anderson implants, Asia wasn't really his type but she gave incredible head, her lips vacuuming the pleasure out of him and making it last and last and last. You could forgive and forget a lot of things if a woman could make you feel like that.

He tuned back into the recording, adjusting the controls to get the balance exactly right. Asia was really into it now, hitting a malacca rod against her thigh to stimulate the swish of a schoolmaster's cane. Her gasps of delicious agony were stimulatingly realistic.

'Oh! Oh! Oh! That feels so strange. It stings so much but

Aurelia Clifford

it feels nice, please don't stop. Oh sir, what's happening to me? I'm all wet between my legs . . .'

If only, thought Kieran. He let his thoughts wander. It wasn't Asia speaking to him through his headphones, it was April Sanchez. They were standing on the sixth floor balcony of the television studios at Albert Dock, and she was half silhouetted against the eggshell blue of a perfect summer sky. She was laughing and pouting, blowing kisses to him as she leaned back against the handrail, rubbing herself against it, thrusting out her breasts, making them dance underneath her white silk vest.

As he watched, she started stripping for him, taking her clothes off slowly and tantalisingly. First her tight red skirt, unzipping it and letting gravity make it slide, at first achingly slowly, down her hips. Then the sleeveless silk vest, which she pulled off over her head to reveal a tiny stretch cotton bra, underwired and edged with lace.

She stooped to pick up the skirt and blouse and, turning away from him, held them over the six floor drop to the dock below.

'. . . Do you want to see more, sir?' purred the voice in Kieran's head.

'Yes. Oh yes, more, much more.'

April's fingers opened and the clothes fell through the hot blue air, tumbling over and over each other as they plummeted towards the water beneath. She turned back to look at him, beautifully irresistible in her white bra and panties, barefoot with summer-gold skin and her mass of jet-black hair pinned up into loose tangles of waves and curls. The nape of her neck was long, smooth,

STRANGERS IN THE NIGHT

bare, too devoid of kisses for Kieran's liking.

'. . . Ask me and I'll do it again . . .'

The voice in his head guided the pictures. Asia's voice but April's body, slender but ripe and oh so fascinatingly juicy. She peeled down her bra straps, reached behind her and unhooked the catch. As she pulled away her bra and discarded it, Kieran saw that her tan was unbroken. He wondered if she sunbathed naked on the flat roof of her apartment block, and the sexual agony was so exquisite that it was almost too much for him to bear . . .

'More, I'm going to do more. Oh sir, take off my panties and do bad things to me. You can put your tongue in my pussy if you like . . .'

He almost ejaculated at the thought, not of Asia Starr but of April Sanchez, bending forward over the balcony rail, inviting him to pull down her panties and take her. In fact, he was so carried away by this seductive idea that he accidentally pressed the wrong button on the control console, setting off a complete different tape.

'Damn.' He waved to Asia through the dividing screen. 'Be with you in a minute. Take a breather.'

He reached over to hit the stop/eject button, when he heard a voice he recognised. The voice of Marsha Fox. Intrigued, he turned up the volume.

'. . . Not just a question of *operational* difficulties. Surely you can see the impossibility of my position?'

Another voice now. A man's, too indistinct to be identifiable, muffled and distant as though he were at the other side of a large room.

'It's not my job to bail you out of trouble.'

83

'I need more time. I *have* to have more time.'

'You've had all the time you're going to get, Marsha. Now are you going to do what you're told?'

Pause.

'Look, April Sanchez has to be got out of the way. And Kieran Harte, too . . .'

'. . . and Kieran Harte, too.'

Marsha's voice cut off abruptly and the end of the tape flicked round and round on the spool, filling the room with an empty clicking sound. Kieran switched off the tape machine. But Marsha Fox's words kept on reverberating round April's flat.

Kieran pushed a lock of sandy hair back from his face.

'Well?'

April met his gaze.

'I've told you before, Kieran, I don't appreciate your sense of humour.'

'You think this is some kind of a *joke*?'

April folded her arms and leaned back against the wall. She looked irresistible like that, thought Kieran. April hadn't always despised him, but the fact of her contempt and her suspicion only served to make him want her more.

'Take you a long time, did it?'

'What?'

'To get all the little bits and splice them together, then record them onto a fresh spool of tape.'

'You think I'd do that?'

'I wouldn't put anything past you, Kieran. You stole my show, remember?'

STRANGERS IN THE NIGHT

Exasperation tore at Kieran's guts. He could have taken April by the shoulders and shaken her. Then again, he could have carried her into the bedroom, thrown her down on the bed Rhett Butler style and dived in like a hot knife into butter . . .

'I've told you till I'm blue in the face, April, I knew nothing about what Marsha was planning, nothing at all! And now God knows what she's cooking up to get rid of us . . .'

April squared up to him, eyes blazing, her body so close that he could breathe in the intoxicating scent of her beneath the veil of expensive perfume.

'You're a liar, Kieran. Anybody could have forged that tape. It's you who are trying to get rid of me. You've wanted me out of Mersey Roar ever since—'

'Grow up, April. Just because you kicked me out of your bed once doesn't turn me into some kind of embittered psycho. Don't you think you're flattering yourself a little too much?'

'You're flattering yourself if you think you can convince me with *that*.'

She jabbed a finger at the spool of tape. Kieran picked it up and slipped it into his jacket pocket.

'Fair enough. Don't say I didn't try.'

'You're leaving?'

'There doesn't seem to be a lot of point in sticking around. But if I were you I'd think about it, April. Whatever you may think about me, I don't want anything bad to happen to you – and this is something that threatens us both.'

85

Something in Kieran's voice made April pause for a moment. Kieran's story was so unconvincing that it had the ring of truth to it. Only Kieran Harte could accidentally overhear a taped conversation in which their boss threatened to have them both 'eliminated'.

'Just supposing I said I believed you . . .'

Kieran allowed himself the ghost of a sarcastic smile.

'Hallelujah.'

'I didn't say I did, just that I might. But just supposing?'

'Well . . . we could work together, try and find out what's going on.'

Silence was thick and dark and heavy in the room. Switching on a table lamp, April walked across to the window and drew the curtains. Dusk was falling over the city.

'I have to leave soon, to do the show.'

'I know.'

There were things that needed to be said. April wondered why she hadn't felt the need to say them before. But then again, she'd avoided being alone with Kieran ever since that disastrous, drunken one-night stand, using her spite and her resentment as a wall between them.

'Kieran . . . I've been getting messages.'

'What kind of messages?'

'Weird ones.' She took a carved wooden box off a shelf and opened it, taking out the cards she had received. 'Dan says they're nothing, I'm not so sure.'

Kieran looked at them, read the message. She pointed to the watch.

'One hundred, ninety nine, ninety eight, it counts

STRANGERS IN THE NIGHT

down – do you see? I counted right down to zero and that falls on the fifteenth of September.'

Kieran felt cold fingers tighten on the back of his neck. For April's sake he tried not to show it but this time he was powerfully, inexplicably afraid.

'Yeah?'

April took the cards and put them back in the box.

'Do you think Marsha Fox . . .?'

'I have no idea.' He made an effort to sound casual. 'You could be right and it's nothing to worry about – some prat's idea of a bad joke. Even someone at a rival station who knows you're damn good and is trying to put you off your stride.' He glanced at his watch. 'It's getting late, I guess I'd better leave. We could talk about this some other time. If you wanted to . . .'

There was something about fear, April realised as she looked at Kieran. Something that could join two people more powerfully than love ever could. Something that could sharpen vague, unfocused lust and turn it into a savage, irresistible force.

'Kieran . . .'

He turned back.

'Hmm?'

She touched his shoulder, very lightly, but a laserbeam of arousal cut through him, stiffening his cock to stone.

'Don't go.'

'You'll be late if I stay.'

'Mike'd cover for me if I asked him to.' April's throat was sandpaper dry, the palms of her hands wet with perspiration. 'Did you mean what you said?'

Aurelia Clifford

'About . . .?'

'About not wanting bad things to happen to me?'

Kieran took her hand and, very slowly and tenderly, carried it to his lips.

'I may be a complete idiot, April. I may be the last man in the world you'd want to go to bed with. But I'm not a liar. I care about you, April. I care about what happens to you, I always have done.'

She tried to control her breathing, but the breaths came in tiny gasps. She was dizzy, sick with anticipation and the realisation of something she had tried for too many months to deny.

'You're . . . not.'

Kieran took the middle finger of her left hand and ran his tongue tip over it, down to the base of her palm and then back to the tip.

'Not what?' he murmured, though he knew the answer. She whispered it, her words shimmering like a heat haze on the summer night air.

'Not the last man in the world I'd want to go to bed with.'

She slid slowly down Kieran's body until she was on her knees, her hands smoothing down his chest, his flanks, his thighs. Under that washed out polo shirt and jeans his body was hard and athletic, the muscles tense and toned beneath the surface of the skin.

His scent was faint but delicious; the light fragrance of sweat on showered skin, the spicy tang of citrus body scrub. As she unfastened the buttons on his 501s, she looked up at him.

STRANGERS IN THE NIGHT

'There's something I've been wanting to do for a long time.'

How long he had wanted her to do it to him, Kieran couldn't remember. In fact he couldn't recall a time when he hadn't wanted April Sanchez with a hot, hard wanting that simply wasn't going to go away. How often had he tried to kill the feeling? Often enough to know that it would never die.

Her fingers were quick and nimble as they unfastened his fly and slipped inside, pushing through into his trunks, sliding between his thighs until they cradled the fat, juicy fruits that ached for her touch. He slid his legs a little further apart, stroking her face as she explored his sex.

April's middle finger slipped softly into the valley between his thighs, skating over the mossy purse of his scrotum and seeking out the incredibly sensitive pathway between the base of his penis and the tight hardness of his anal sphincter. She knew just how to do it, lightly scratching her fingernail over his flesh, beginning between his buttocks and drawing it forward with terrible slowness.

The anticipation of pleasure was every bit as good as the pleasure itself, the shiver of expectation tensing his balls and drawing them in closer to his body. They fitted perfectly into the cupped palm of her hand as she brought her hand forward and began squeezing them, rolling and palpating them in the coolness of her hand.

With her other hand she began to stroke his belly, smoothing fingers and palm over the tiny sandy-coloured hairs that led in a meandering line from navel to pubis. They lay flat against his skin but she erected them, rubbing his skin against the lie of the hairs, then pressing her lips to his belly and teasing them with the very tip of her tongue.

Kieran thought he might perhaps be in paradise. He wasn't sure. It was difficult to be sure of anything when April Sanchez was kissing and licking your belly, her hands caressing your testicles while she trailed cool, cool saliva over your overheated flesh.

A pulse of desire thumped through his body, making the stiff baton of his prick dance and jerk against his belly. Could she feel the beat of his lust through her cheek, pressed close to his skin? Was that same pulse of need echoed in her own body?

The kisses stopped at the base of his cock, circling but not touching it. It seemed to burn and ache. April knelt back and looked up at Kieran.

'Do you want me?'

'You know I do.'

'How much?'

'Enough to drive me insane if I don't have you.'

'Tell me, Kieran. Tell me *exactly* what you want.'

He was mesmerised by her lips, dark and purplish red with smeared lipstick. He'd never seen her quite like this before, dishevelled and wild. She looked dangerously carnivorous, and he imagined those lips parting to reveal a double row of sharp white teeth.

'I want you . . . to suck me dry.'

Out of the dark O of her mouth came the pink stamen of her tongue, muscular and wet with saliva. She ran her tongue slowly and lasciviously up the whole length of his shaft, beginning at the swell of his balls and ending by

STRANGERS IN THE NIGHT

lapping at the beads of clear moisture oozing from his cock tip.

'You taste good.' She smiled. 'You make me want more.'

April engulfed him with a kind of controlled hunger; not suddenly but with a long, slow swallow that took his cock between her lips, slid it across her tongue and deep into the hot, wet gorge of her throat. Her fingers tightened about his balls, imprisoning him in a cage of erotic bliss. Escape? Who would be mad enough to want to escape from this?

Her breathing grew shallower and quickened slightly, setting the rhythm for their joyride. Kieran stroked the underside of her throat and felt the smooth, peristaltic movements as she sucked at his cock. This didn't just feel good, this felt like a fantasy come true. And April Sanchez had been his fantasy for longer than he could remember.

Suddenly the urge for control swept over him. He seized April's head and held it firm as he began to thrust into her mouth. She was quivering, he could feel her whole body shaking; and her mouth was filling with hot saliva that slooshed and trickled over his glans as he thrust in, in, in, taking what he had to have and now.

April scarcely recognised her lover as the Kieran she knew. Tonight he was hot, hard, dominant, and she liked him this way; liked him more than she'd have believed possible. The near brutal urgency of his thrusts half choked her but she pushed back against his dick, taking it deeper and deeper, showing him that her desire was every bit as strong as his.

She ached for him, her underclothes wet with excitement, her clitoris rubbing gently against the strip of lace that had worked its way between the petals of her sex. Moving her hips from side to side she intensified the pleasure, masturbating herself as she took Kieran closer to the moment of no turning back. There was a familiar hot heaviness between her thighs, a concentration of heat, a second's hesitation and then an explosion of satisfied lust.

As she swayed, momentarily dizzy with satisfaction, she felt him tremble on her tongue. A quivering, expectant moment; and then Kieran's cock began to jerk and spurt, filling her throat with the all consuming taste of his pleasure.

It was breakfast time when April got back home from the studio. Unlocking the front door of her flat, she saw a familiar pink envelope waiting for her on the doormat.

Another card. She hesitated before bending to pick it up, annoyed with herself for being afraid of something that was probably nothing at all, some obsessed fan's sick obsession.

Tearing open the envelope, she slid out the card. It showed the same picture as before, the White Rabbit holding the stopwatch which as she'd expected read '96'. Only there was one thing different about the picture, one tiny thing that hit the eye and demanded its attention.

A bright red noose, hanging from the White Rabbit's neck.

Chapter 6

The following afternoon, April met Kieran for lunch at a waterside restaurant just outside Chester.

'What next, that's the question.'

Kieran nodded and pushed his food around his plate. He liked king prawns with ginger, but just lately he seemed to be losing his appetite for everything except April Sanchez.

'You didn't mind coming all the way out here to eat? It seemed safer somehow.'

Their eyes met. Both were thinking about last night. Had it really happened? April was first to look away, her gaze following a red and yellow dinghy as it glided round a bend in the river. There were two people in it, a young man in a white shirt and trousers and a girl in a floaty dress. Lovers, that was pretty obvious from the way they were kissing. They even had a bottle of wine in an ice bucket, and a picnic hamper. Kieran followed her gaze with an ironic smile.

'They get the smoked salmon and champagne, and we get the death threats. Seems fair enough, wouldn't you say?'

As long as I get you, he added silently in the privacy of his thoughts. Despite what had happened last night, despite the raw, urgent sex that had made April half an hour late for the start of her show, despite all that . . . he still wasn't sure of her, couldn't tell what she really thought or felt. Things had seemed easier in the darkness, somehow. A woman's sex, slick with honeysweet juice, doesn't lie to you.

April reached for the wine bottle at precisely the same moment as Kieran. Their hands touched, drew back, fumbled with crumbs on the tablecloth. It was true what people said: sex did complicate things. After you'd made love with someone, there could be no going back to the way things were before.

'Last night, April—'

'Let's not talk about last night.'

'We'll have to talk about it sometime.'

'Perhaps. But not right now. Right now the question is – what do we do next?'

'We find out what's happening. And why.'

'How?'

'I'm not sure. Together?'

Something inside April made her draw back. She didn't understand why, not after what had happened between them, but it was there all the same. Perhaps *because* of what had happened.

'Slow down, Kieran. What are you saying – that we're some kind of item? Because if you are—'

Kieran put up his hand. If he was honest it wasn't any easier for him than it was for April – except for the fact

STRANGERS IN THE NIGHT

that he, at least, knew what he wanted.

'I'm not saying anything, just that there are two of us and if we work together we're going to get further faster.'

April was regretting her outburst already. When all was said and done the desire that had drawn her and Kieran together the previous night was still there, burning and bubbling just under the surface – and maybe that was why it was so awkward between them right now. If she'd been less strung out maybe she'd have asked him to take her to bed and make it all right again . . .

'Yeah. OK, you're right. So what do we do?'

'Find out who's behind all this. We know Marsha Fox has something to do with it, because of the tape – but what? And then there's Sven Harlesson . . .'

'Sven? But he's a victim. He's practically turned into a basket case since all that shit came out about him.'

'True. But *why*? Why would anybody target him?'

'Because he's an easy target?'

'Could be. I still think he might be able to give us some kind of lead. Besides, what else do we have?'

'Not much,' admitted April, refilling her wine glass almost to the brim. 'OK. I'll see how close I can get to Marsha, find out what she knows. And you'll take care of Sven?'

Kieran raised an eyebrow. 'Gee thanks.'

'I shouldn't worry, you're not really his type.'

'You'll be careful, won't you? With Marsha.' Kieran's hand gripped the back of April's wrist.

'Naturally.'

'Don't trust her, whatever you do.'

'Don't worry, I won't.'

Kieran's touch was uncomfortably possessive, but it still took an effort of will to detach herself from it and look into those cobalt-blue eyes. The question is, she thought to herself, can I trust you?

What goes around comes around, thought Kieran. And tonight it was his turn to file a news report on 'Battle of the Bands'.

Tonight's round was one of the quarter finals, held not in the studios but at Minsky's Rave Club, a stone's throw from the Cavern. And to judge from the quality of what he'd seen so far, thought Kieran, stone throwing was a definite possibility before the night was out. Not that the audience seemed to care. Maybe they were all high on something, at any rate a swarm of jiggling, giggling, Spandex-covered bodies rushed the stage every time the curtains twitched.

Mike Meen was MCing as usual, Sven propping up the bar with three empty pint glasses lined up in front of him. He was drinking snakebite with double vodkas, and if he carried on like this he'd be waking up in bed with a stomach pump.

In a break between bands, Mike Meen came down from the stage, pushing his way through the crowd to the bar. He had had a new haircut, thought Kieran. A seriously trendy haircut, razorcut and streaked golden blond. The woolly tanktop had been displaced by a cool leather jacket which almost but not quite hid his middle age spread.

STRANGERS IN THE NIGHT

'Hi there, Kieran – enjoying the gig?'

'Yeah – great.' He hoped he sounded convincing enough, but Mike was sufficiently carried away not to notice. Where *did* he find these bands?

'What did you think of Axehead?' Mike nodded towards the stage.

Kieran cast his mind back two acts, to the four school-boys with hair extensions.

'Um . . . what did *you* think of them? You're the hard rock expert.'

It was the right thing to say. Mike beamed modestly.

'Oh I don't know . . . mind you, I do know a thing or two about music, I've been around long enough to know talent when I see it. And mark my words, Kieran, this year's contest is going to produce at least one top band for the twenty-first century. Axehead are good, but Vanilla-Sex . . . just wait till you catch them in the semis.'

Mike caught Kieran's gaze and followed it to Sven Harlesson, miserably crouched over the bar with his hands cradling yet another glass.

'Poor bastard,' he observed. 'He's cracking up. Still, I suppose our past always catches up with us in the end.'

Kieran observed him sharply.

'So what's going to catch up with you, that we don't know about?'

Mike squirmed for a fleeting moment, then laughed, a little too jovially.

'Nice line, Kieran, I like it. Maybe I'll use it in the show sometime.'

Kieran watched Mike climb back on the stage and

announce a guest band for the interval entertainment. He didn't catch the name of the act, but no problem, if they were any good (or spectacularly crap) he could find that out later.

At least they'd bothered to look interesting, if a little passé. White faced ghouls in black leather, their lead singer dressed like an old-style undertaker with a tailcoat and a black chiffon scarf trailing from his top hat. Black ringed eyes and black lipstick made them look a bit like Alice Cooper's psychotic cousins. They had a dancer with them, too: a skinny girl in a skeleton mask and black leather bikini. Macabre was the only word Kieran could think of to describe them.

The first thunderous chords gave way to a thumping beat. *Run, Rabbit, Run*? Was he imagining it? No, the tune was definitely there, though almost swamped by grungy guitars. And the words weren't how he remembered them either – something about graveyards, very spooky and unsettling.

He could only make out the odd word here and there, but then the chorus crashed in, and suddenly he wondered if he'd slipped through a hole in reality into some nightmarish basement.

'Run Kieran, run Kieran, run, run, run . . .'

What?

'. . . There's a bullet in your head and you're very, very dead . . . so run Kieran, run Kieran, run, run, run . . .'

Bloody hell. He *wasn't* imagining it. Or the look in those black rimmed eyes – they were staring right at him and

STRANGERS IN THE NIGHT

laughing. The girl in the mask and the bikini was jiggling and writhing as if she was in a trance, the disjointed bony arms and legs jerking, her scrawny breasts jumping inside the tight leather bra.

The weird thing about it all, the *really* weird thing, was that nobody else seemed to have noticed the song lyrics. The audience were jumping and jerking too, laughing and dancing, lost in the music. And after the contest, when Kieran started asking questions, nobody would admit to knowing the guest band's name. They weren't even on the bill for the evening.

No band. No name. No nothing. It was as if they'd never existed.

April handed her invitation to a toastmaster in red and gold livery, and walked through onto the terrace.

It was a warm evening, and the cocktail party at the French Consulate was well attended. A string quartet was performing in the ballroom behind her, waiters were gliding around silently with trays of champagne and canapés decorated with thin black slivers of truffle, women with immaculate hair and thousand pound dresses were carrying on exquisitely meaningless conversations with businessmen, diplomats and the occasional media celebrity. No wonder April had had to pull strings to get an invitation. The French Consulate wasn't accustomed to guests like April Sanchez.

She knew all eyes were on her the moment she stepped into the party. Heads turned, conversation faltered for a few seconds and then began again as the guests remembered

Aurelia Clifford

their manners and pretended not to stare. April supposed that they had a right to stare. After all, however much of an effort she'd made to look good, she couldn't bring herself to look conventional. There were just so many compromises a woman could make, and then no more.

The invitation had made it clear that long evening gowns were a must. So April had borrowed one – from a friend of hers who was a hostess in a fetishwear club. It was a divine creation in purple glove leather, so soft and supple that as it warmed, it moulded itself precisely to the wearer's body.

The low-cut bodice was boned, emphasising April's small waist and throwing her breasts forward, making them look much larger than they really were. The skirt was gored, sewn from eight separate triangular sections which clung tightly at the hips then flared out. As she walked her skirt swirled about her legs, the panels slashed to the thigh so that if she made a sudden turn they flew out like the petals of some sultry Eastern flower. Underneath she was wearing a silk thong and suspenders, teamed with pale golden stockings which shimmered as they caught the light from the chandeliers.

Head up, she took a glass from the tray offered to her, and walked serenely through the crowd. This was a new experience, a new opportunity to be outrageous, and it was giving her a buzz she hadn't experienced since her sixteenth birthday. That day, for a dare, she'd played cello in the school orchestra without any knickers on, and made absolutely sure that the drop dead gorgeous

STRANGERS IN THE NIGHT

music master got a *very* good look before somebody'd grassed on her to the Head.

Without turning to look, she knew that she was being watched. She could feel the eyes on her. Some were critical, others curious, many lustful and caressing. How many of the people here desired her, how many wondered what this outrageous young woman might look like stripped of her gown and panties, kneeling doggy style on the Parian marble floor, her gloved hands holding her buttocks wide apart to reveal the irresistible lure of her sex . . .?

The thought made her feel more sexy than ever. There were good looking men here and some of them were trying to catch her eye. But tempting as they were, that was not what she'd come for. She'd come here to find someone in particular. Someone called Marsha Fox.

As it turned out, Marsha saw her first. April felt a hand touch her arm.

'April? April Sanchez, it *is* you! What on earth . . .?'

April turned round slowly and confronted Marsha with a smile. Marsha was looking good tonight with her tight black sheath dress and diamond drop earrings, very good indeed; but not as good as April Sanchez was feeling tonight.

'Hello, Marsha. Enjoying the party?'

Marsha took a sip of champagne.

'Well, well, April. I wouldn't have thought this was your kind of thing at all.'

'Really?' April felt serene, sexy, completely in control. 'You'd be surprised.' She lowered her voice. 'In fact there are a lot of things you don't know about me, Marsha.'

101

Aurelia Clifford

Her smile drew Marsha in. April knew the chemistry was unmistakably there between them, the same spark which had ignited that day in Marsha's office at Mersey Roar.

'So it seems.'

April ran her fingers down Marsha's arm. Even through her silky evening glove she could feel a quiver of appreciation pass through the older woman's body.

'Perhaps you'd like to know more? There's so much more I'd like to show you.'

Without waiting for Marsha's reply, April set off across the terrace towards the gardens which stretched out behind the Consulate. At this time of night they were in darkness, save for the white lamps which had been hooked onto high branches of the trees, creating pools of light and shadow among the flowerbeds and foliage.

The grass was soft and springy underfoot. April walked slowly away from the noise and brightness of the party, wondering how long it would be before Marsha's curiosity got the better of her.

Marsha caught her up as she walked through the rose arbour into a secluded clearing with a sunken pond and fountain.

'What is this all about, April?'

April took her time replying, her exhilaration suddenly mingled with the adrenalin rush of apprehension. This might turn out to be a dangerous game, but she wanted to play it anyhow. In the lamplight Marsha's eyes shone yellow as a cat's.

STRANGERS IN THE NIGHT

'It's about you and me, Marsha. But then, you know that already, don't you?'

She heard the hiss of indrawn breath.

'April . . .'

'You felt it too. That day in your office. You would have kissed me if Kieran Harte hadn't barged in.'

'Oh? What makes you think that?'

'I don't think, Marsha. I *know*. You're just as tired of playing games as I am.'

She moved closer. Now they were almost touching.

'Why don't you do it now, Marsha? I know you want to.'

Afterwards, April wondered how she had dared do it. How she had ever found the courage to challenge Marsha Fox. Does the mouse ask the cat for a dance? But tonight the madness of lust was inside April and she would have done anything. Tonight this wasn't about investigating what was happening, this was about the satisfaction of a sexual impulse.

'Well, well, April. I'm so glad you've decided to see things my way at last.'

Marsha's fingernails were long and metallic silver. They dug hard into April's shoulders as she pulled her close and captured her in a predatory kiss. At the end of it they were both breathless and panting.

'You wore this dress to torment me.'

'Yes.'

'You planned this, didn't you, April? You came here especially to dare me to seduce you.'

'Make love to me, Marsha. I'll die if you don't make love to me tonight.'

Aurelia Clifford

April had tried most sexual experiments in her time, but it was a long, long time since she had felt another woman's hands on her, stripping her, undressing her with the caresses that only a woman understands. There they were in the garden of the Consulate, no more than a hundred yards from the party, ripping each other's clothes off, getting gloriously naked in the hot summer night.

The grass was spattered with tiny droplets of icy water which had splashed out from the fountain. The contrast of hot earth and cold water made April gasp as she sank to the ground with the weight of Marsha's body across her flank.

Marsha's breasts were plump and heavy upon her belly, their nipples hard stalks which traced circles and spirals on her skin as they trembled and swung.

'You're a slut, April. A filthy minded slut.'

'Can I help being what I am?' April took Marsha's hands and guided them to her breasts. 'Feel how hard my nipples are for you. It's not my fault. This is what you've done to me.'

Marsha murmured her pleasure as she bent lower over April's body and planted tiny lovebites all over her small, firm breasts. All the while, her thigh was sliding between April's legs, its athletic hardness rubbing rhythmically against the swollen mound of her sex. April's womanhood opened up like some night-blossoming orchid and sweetness flooded out, heavy scented and glossy, slippery as sun warmed oil as it smeared over Marsha's thigh.

April lay back and slid her legs a little further apart. Kneeling over her, a living bronze statue in the twilight,

STRANGERS IN THE NIGHT

Marsha rewarded her with a harder thrust of her thigh, rubbing not with violence but firmly, unforgivingly, making April respond to the thousand mingled sensations trembling from her swollen clitoris.

She reached up. A fine mist of cool water was falling onto her body from the mouth of a stone dolphin. It tingled as it touched her palm, and she stretched out her moistened fingers, transferring the wet coolness to the pendulous warmth of Marsha's breasts.

Marsha let out a little mew of contentment and took hold of April's hand, pulling it down her body to the shadowed triangle at the base of her belly. A thrill of excitement ran through April. The flesh was plump as only a woman's sex can be.

'Put your fingers inside me, April. Finger me.'

The inner lips of Marsha's sex were swamp wet and sticky, so delectable that once April had plunged in she longed to go further and further and deeper. And she was certainly in deep, there was no doubt about that. Perhaps even deeper than she'd meant to be.

'I was wondering, April. Have you ever tried sex with another woman?'

April's heart missed a beat. Surely Dan couldn't have found out about what she and Marsha had done at the party . . . It took an effort to sound innocently curious.

'Why do you ask?'

Dan Lauren was sitting in his office at Viper Sounds, his boots casually resting on the desk. He swung his feet onto the floor and stood up.

105

Aurelia Clifford

'Because the thought of it turns me on, that's why. I have this recurring fantasy that I'm watching you getting it on with another woman, and then joining in.'

'And you think I'd go along with that, do you?'

Dan laughed. It was a warm sound, and the corners of his eyes crinkled when he smiled, softening the extreme darkness of those glittering black diamonds. He slid his hands round April's waist and pulled her closer.

'I think . . . no, I *know*, that you're completely insatiable. Why would a sensible girl like you deny herself a new source of pleasure?'

'Ah, but why should I tell you all my secrets?'

'Because they're not really secrets at all? Look, what I don't know about you I can guess, April. You live for sex, and I give you the best sex you've ever had.'

'You're an arrogant son of a bitch, Dan Lauren.'

'Not arrogant, April. Just wildly successful, absurdly talented and magnificently rich. Don't you think I have every right to think of myself as the best?'

April glanced around the walls of Dan's office. In a way he was right. You could hardly make out the colour of the emulsion under the patchwork of gold and platinum discs, awards and citations, mementoes of rock legends, and press photographs of Dan Lauren fronting Outside My Shadow, being outrageous as only he could be.

He chuckled as he saw April looking at a newspaper photograph from five or six years earlier.

'Remember that night, April?'

'That was a long time before I met you.'

'Sure. But you saw it all on TV, didn't you? By the next

STRANGERS IN THE NIGHT

morning practically the whole world knew about my new "art foundation".'

April recalled the TV images, still crisp as newly minted ten-pound notes in her memory.

'Yeah, well it's not every day a rock singer buys a Picasso original, takes it to the end of Brighton Pier and puts a match to it. Most people thought you were criminally insane.'

'And you, April? What did you think?'

'I thought you were the cleverest man alive. No one but you could have dreamed up a publicity stunt like that.'

Dan encircled her with his arms and pushed her hard against the wall. She felt the chill from the cold, emulsioned plaster seeping through her shirt and pants to her breasts and belly. Dan bit tiny sharp kisses into the smooth scoop of her neck.

'That was the night you first wanted me to screw you. Wasn't it, April?'

She wriggled, her ribcage squashed by the force of his caresses, the weight of his body full up against her back and buttocks.

'Dan, Dan don't – I can't breathe!'

She heard the soft zizz of a zipper. Then Dan's voice, softly ironic.

'Don't bullshit me. If you can talk you can breathe.'

'Not here, Dan – your secretary might come in. Someone might find us.'

The cold hardness of the wall was making her body ache, turning flesh to gooseflesh and the soft discs of her nipples to ice pink cones. It wasn't the threat of discovery she was frightened of, it was the danger of giving in to her own weakness – and the danger that sexual excitement or guilt or both might drive her to tell Dan everything about Kieran . . . and Marsha Fox.

'Answer me, April. You wanted me to screw you, didn't you?'

His hand slid between her belly and the wall, releasing the button on her tight leather trousers. The zipper gave way and he wrenched them down with one hand, the other moving up to her breast, crushing and pinching it, making her want things that frightened her a little. She trembled at the pleasure of Dan's urgent hunger. Could he read the betrayal in her thoughts? Did he know what she had done . . . with Kieran Harte, with Marsha Fox . . .?

'Y-e-e-e-s. Yes, Dan. I wanted you – but I was just a schoolkid then, I never really thought we'd get together . . .'

Dan had pulled her trousers down over her buttocks and they were about halfway down her thighs. April wasn't in the habit of wearing underwear with trousers, she preferred the smooth line of naked flesh under leather and the tease of the centre seam tickling her bare pussy lips. Her breasts were crushed up hard against the wall but her buttocks were thrust slightly back. They fitted wonderfully easily into Dan Lauren's hands.

'I don't believe that for a moment, April. You're an ambitious woman, a sensual woman. What you want you go for. It's no mistake we met at the Varga Club that night. You knew I'd be there, you found out what I like, and you dressed especially for me.' His two hands gripped her

STRANGERS IN THE NIGHT

buttocks, forcing them wide apart. 'Black leather and shiny knee boots. You always know how to turn me on.'

Dan's thumbs explored the territory they were about to conquer. April felt unbelievably exposed, there were no secrets left to her. Her buttocks were spread wide, pulling open the gaping mouth of her sex and making the tight eye of her anus blink and quiver.

'Oh. Oh Dan . . .'

Her inner sex was covered with thick, syrupy wetness. She felt Dan scoop some of it up and smear it all along the deep valley between her pubis and the base of her spine. He repeated the action again and again, until she was soaked with her own wetness.

The first touch of his thumbnails on her sphincter made her writhe with embarrassed pleasure. She wasn't repressed, truly she wasn't, but he'd never done this to her before, never shown quite such an obvious delight in confusing pleasure with pain.

The caresses were rough but skilful. The sharpness of Dan's nails scratched over the thin membrane of April's arse, occasionally digging deeper or pushing a little way inside the tightly-puckered ring of muscle.

'You're beautifully tight,' he murmured, his fingers tightening around the flesh of her buttocks as his thumbs coaxed her to open up this last secret to him. 'But you're opening up to me, you know that, don't you? It's no use trying to hide your pleasure from me.'

The slick lubricant made it all too simple for Dan to penetrate her with a sharp diving movement of his two thumbs, pushing them inside her simultaneously. The sensation was so sudden and so savage that April was certain he would tear her apart. He pushed harder into her, further and deeper, all the time widening the distance between his thumbs so that he was stretching and dilating her.

'Let yourself go, April. Relax.'

She was opening up, blossoming, turning into some crazy flower dancing on the double stalk that pushed deeper and deeper into the moist coolness of her calyx. The sensation was half pleasure, half pain; equally divided between the incredible spreading warmth of wanting and the fear-tinged agony of feeling her flesh stretch and almost give way.

His dick slid easily into the soft glove of her sex. Only the thinnest of membranes separated Dan's penis and his thumbs, still working away at her, annihilating any small trace of resistance.

Suddenly hungry, she threw back her hips and met his cockthrust, burying him to the balls in her sweet softness.

'Feels good. Feels . . . incredible.'

Dan speared her again and again, using his hands to pull her hard onto his cock then pushing her forward so that her breasts and the side of her cheek met the cold wall.

'Tell me how it feels. *Exactly* how it feels.'

'Like being taken over, possessed. Like owning nothing that's mine any more. I can't see your face . . .'

'You don't need to see. Just feel.'

'It's like . . . having sex with a stranger. A complete stranger.'

STRANGERS IN THE NIGHT

Dan's fingernails bit deep into April's flesh. She could feel the tension in his body, smell the excitement of him. He was close to orgasm but she was closer, surfing the biggest wave of all . . .

'Nothing is more liberating than being a stranger,' whispered Dan. 'When no one knows who you are, you can do anything, get away with anything. And no one in the world can touch you . . .

'Unless you want to be touched.'

Chapter 7

It was about a week later that Sven Harlesson didn't turn up for work. Which meant that 'Drivetime with Sven' suddenly turned into 'Drivetime with Kieran'. Kieran was not impressed.

'Marsha, this isn't good enough. Why can't somebody else do Sven's show? Correction, why can't he do it himself?'

Marsha gave him a sweet, butter wouldn't melt, sort of look.

'Kieran *darling*, you and I both know that Sven has a few personal problems at the moment.'

'You mean he spends most of his time pissed out of his brain and sobbing into his beer? Look, Marsha, it's not that I'm unsympathetic . . .'

She leaned across the desk and patted the back of his hand. Tenderness from Marsha Fox was not so much reassuring as disconcerting.

'Do it just for today, Kieran. For me. Overtime rates of course, and I'm sure Sven will be back tomorrow.'

'He'd better be,' was Kieran's parting shot as he

113

slammed the door shut behind him and stomped off down the stairs.

It was about six thirty when he emerged from the studio. His neck ached and he was losing his voice, but at least he was free until tomorrow. He'd better make a fast getaway before Marsha decided he could stand in for somebody else.

Slipping on his jacket, he went down through Reception. Sherrie was waving goodbye to two girls in matching Bermuda shorts.

'Oh hi, Kieran – sweet isn't it? They met through "Strangers in the Night" and came to invite April to their Humanist wedding.'

'How touching. Knowing April, she'll probably go.' He checked his pigeonhole. 'Don't suppose you've heard anything from Sven?'

'He hasn't rung in.' She lowered her voice. 'He had a skinful last night, I expect he's sleeping it off.'

'Maybe I'll call in on him on the way home.'

It wasn't really altruism that made Kieran drive round to Sven's house, though he couldn't help sympathising with the bloke. The overriding impulse was to make sure that Sven was awake, sober and on his feet; and stayed that way long enough to do his show tomorrow.

Number twelve Hawthorn Street stood bang in the middle of a neat terrace in one of the smarter parts of town. Kieran walked through the painted wooden gate and rang the bell, keeping his finger on it for several seconds. As he'd expected, nobody came to the door. Sven's lover Graham was often away for days at a time,

STRANGERS IN THE NIGHT

and Sven was no doubt comatose on his bed with a couple of empty brandy bottles for company.

Luckily he'd been to the house before and knew that Sven kept a spare key under the terracotta strawberry planter in the back yard. It was easy to find it, unlock the back door and step into the kitchen. New Age music was playing somewhere in the background, but there was no sign of life.

'Sven? Wakey wakey Sven, this is your evening wake up call.'

No one answered, but that wasn't particularly surprising. Kieran started up the stairs to the bedrooms, following the sound of dolphins and synthesised guitars. He'd got about halfway up when the smell hit him. A horrible, sweet, sickly smell mixed with something worse. What *was* that smell?

There was a door at the top of the stairs. It stood ajar. Before he pushed it open, Kieran had a horrible apprehension of what he would find behind it.

'Oh Sven. Sven, you poor bugger.'

The sight would remain with him forever. You couldn't shut the sight of death out of your mind, it was like an acid etching on silver plate, indelible and sharp. But one thing struck him more than anything else, imprinted on his thoughts as he raced downstairs to telephone the police.

And that was the scarlet noose hanging from Sven's dead throat.

Since the night of the party, something had changed forever between April and Marsha Fox.

115

On the face of it, Marsha was every bit as pushy and unpleasant as she had always been, making sure that everyone at Mersey Roar saw her treating April Sanchez the way she treated everyone else. Like dirt on the sole of her expensive shoe. But it was very strange, the way they just kept 'bumping into' each other, even though their working hours scarcely coincided. Somehow, no matter what time April arrived at the station, she would find Marsha working overtime, or 'just popping in' to check up on something and have a casual cup of coffee.

April had reached the stage where nothing was clear in her mind any more. Incredibly and embarrassingly, she had acquired three lovers: Dan Lauren, Kieran Harte and Marsha Fox. Kieran was the only one of the three who knew exactly what was going on between the four of them – or at least, April hoped so. There was danger in Marsha's dark brown eyes; and Dan Lauren could be completely and exquisitely ruthless with anyone he considered to be his enemy.

This was a suicidal game she was playing, but like an idiot she kept coming back for more, never quite satisfied, always begging for more, never quite sure which – if any of them – she could trust. And in time the danger became a drug, filling her with an intense buzz of sensual excitement she had never experienced before.

A few days after the party, Marsha invited her to her house for dinner, 'to discuss your career, April *darling*.'

'I'm . . . not sure I can manage tonight.'

Marsha's eyes flashed. 'Oh, I think you can.'

'But I've—'

STRANGERS IN THE NIGHT

'Cancel it. I'll see you around seven thirty, you won't be late, will you?'

As she dressed for dinner, April thought about Kieran. Where was he now? She'd only caught sight of him briefly, arguing in the corridor with Marsha about having to sit in for Sven that afternoon. Was he with some other woman tonight – and how would she feel about it if he was? She thought about him screwing that blonde tart – Asia, was it? – having her across the studio console, pulling down her knickers, making her sit down on his cock . . .

The image changed abruptly to one of Kieran with Marsha, Marsha on her knees in her underwear and Kieran making her suck him off. She smiled. Hardly. From all the available evidence, Kieran Harte wasn't Marsha's type at all, and Marsha certainly wasn't the sort to be bossed around by a man. Any man.

Was *she* Marsha's type? She admired her reflection in the mirror. Her friend was heavily into fetishwear, and had recommended this outfit as perfect for a seduction scene – but who was seducing whom?

Was it over the top, had she gone too far? The boots were black PVC with four-inch spiky heels and pointed toes. They extended well above her knees, making way for three inches of fishnet stocking leading up to black rubber hotpants, a strapless bustier in see-through black lace, and a loose collar of silver chains. Red elbow-length gloves completed the look. All she needed was a platinum wig to look like the world's sleaziest, sexiest, most sensual tart.

Marsha's house was on an exclusive development in

Aurelia Clifford

Curzon Park, the home of Chester's most prestigious postcode. As April parked her five year old Nissan outside, she checked the address Marsha had given her. There was no mistake. But how in God's name could Marsha Fox afford to live *here*?

The house was a modern Lutyens pastiche, all mullioned windows and black and white plasterwork. The driveway seemed to go on forever, meandering between sculpted flowerbeds and lawns that looked as if they had been groomed with nail scissors.

The front door opened just as she reached it.

'Good evening, madam.'

April almost fell over with astonishment. 'I . . .'

'Please come in, madam. The Mistress is waiting for you.'

The young man was everything a servant should be: nice manners, tall and good looking, consummately efficient. Conventional he was not. His black hair was gelled into short spikes and he wore a ring through his nose, joined to a long silver chain which divided below his chin and led to smaller rings which passed through his bare nipples.

His olive skin was deeply tanned and there was plenty of it on view. Tattoos of a bird of paradise and a dragon glistened on well oiled shoulders, and a red and green serpent wound down his bare chest to disappear beneath a tiny leather apron. As he turned to lead the way into the house, April saw that this was very nearly all that he was wearing: his perfect golden buttocks were naked save for the thin black string of a thong, disappearing into the

STRANGERS IN THE NIGHT

deep cleft between them. Long, athletic legs led down to bare feet and three gold bracelets on each ankle, which jingled faintly as he walked.

April studied him with interest. To say the least, he was not what she'd expected. Perhaps Marsha Fox's life held other fascinating secrets still to be revealed.

At the other end of the lavishly carpeted corridor, Marsha's servant stopped in front of a door and knocked. After a long pause, a voice answered: 'Enter.'

He stood aside to let April walk in ahead of him. Marsha Fox was stretched out like an empress on a soft white sofa, her body alluringly curvaceous in a Westwood original. The tight laced fur trimmed corset and latex leggings suited her voluptuous figure, highlighting the generous curve of her backside and the creamy pale swell of her breasts, which seemed to threaten to fall out of their tightly moulded cups. As she rolled onto her side with a smile of greeting, April noticed the tiny tattoo of a scarlet devil, nestling on the upswell of her breast.

'April, *sweet girl*, how lovely to see you.' Marsha snapped her fingers. 'Bring more champagne for my guest, and this time make sure that it is properly iced.'

'Yes, mistress.' He inclined his head respectfully and disappeared through a door into a kitchenette.

'Who . . .?'

'His name is Marco. Isn't he exquisite?'

'He seems very efficient,' hazarded April.

Marsha laughed delightedly at this. Curling up her knees, she made room for April at the end of the immense white sofa.

119

Aurelia Clifford

'True. But efficiency is not his most valuable attribute. Don't try to tell me you haven't noticed his . . . other assets.'

April sat down at the end of the sofa. It was luxuriously deep and yielding.

'I didn't think you were interested in men.'

Marsha studied her face with interest, as though she were just realising something.

'Now I understand. You're *jealous*! You're jealous because I lust after Marco as well as you.'

April coloured.

'That's . . . rubbish.'

'If you say so.' Marsha watched Marco returning from the kitchen with an ice bucket and two champagne flutes. 'You are very slow today, Marco,' she scolded.

'I am sorry if my behaviour offends you, mistress.' Marco set down the ice bucket with its bottle of champagne, and arranged the glasses on a coffee table. 'Are you going to punish me?'

'Perhaps.' Marsha's lips twitched with satisfied pleasure. 'If your behaviour continues to be less than satisfactory.' She nodded to Marco. 'You may pour – and make sure that not a drop is spilt.'

April was intrigued by Marco, by the very idea that a man could accept such a subservient role. She smiled at him as he poured her drink.

'Thank you.'

'Don't thank him!' snapped Marsha. 'He's here to be punished, not to be praised. He's my body slave, aren't you, Marco?'

120

STRANGERS IN THE NIGHT

'Yes, mistress.'

'You would do anything for me?'

'Anything at all, mistress.'

Marsha glanced down at her feet, picked up her glass and threw champagne over her high-heeled ankle boots.

'These boots are dirty,' she announced. 'Clean them.'

Marco sank to his knees on the carpet.

'At once, mistress.'

'With your tongue. Quickly now, I'm waiting.'

He lapped so eagerly at the wet patent leather that April couldn't take her eyes off him.

'Wherever did you find him?'

'At the Stock Exchange, would you believe. He was working as a financial dealer, but he wasn't happy, were you, Marco?'

Marco didn't answer, but his soft brown eyes hung on every word like a spaniel unsure if it will receive kicks or kisses. And all the while, his long pink tongue lapped at the patent leather boots, sliding down the uppers and winding about the long black spike of the heel.

'A *financial dealer*?'

'I admit you'd never know it now, April, but that's because Marco was a square peg in a round hole. His temperament was completely wrong, he couldn't take the responsibility and the pressure. He's found his true vocation now, as my slave. All he ever has to do is obey.' Suddenly tiring of Marco's attentions, she kicked him away. 'Enough. Go to your corner.'

Marco crawled away on hands and knees, and crouched beneath a picture which April could have sworn was a

121

Chagall. Where on earth did Marsha get her money – and her energy?

'Put on your mask.'

'Yes, mistress.'

April watched Marco pick up a leather blindfold and tie it over his eyes.

'Can you see anything?'

'No, mistress.'

'Good.'

Marsha swung her feet onto the floor and sat up. Her fingers toyed with the black fishnet stocking which covered April's right thigh.

'Obedience makes him happy. The more obedient he is, the better he pleases me. And the better he pleases me, the more generous and indulgent I am towards him.'

'It seems to work.'

'Oh it does. It does.' Marsha's fingers slid higher up April's thigh. 'And it could work for you, too.'

April caught Marsha's fingers, stopping them dead.

'What do you mean?'

Marsha's face registered hurt.

'Don't push me away, April. All I want to do is make you happy . . . and keep you safe.'

April slid away and got to her feet.

'I'm not Marco. I'm not your toy, Marsha.'

Marsha was right behind her, her breath warm on the back of her neck.

'Of course not. You look wonderful tonight, April. Wonderfully sexy. Won't you kiss and make up?'

Her touch on April's arm made her start with

STRANGERS IN THE NIGHT

unwilling pleasure. There was sensuality in that touch and it was very hard to resist. She half turned to look at Marsha.

'Why do you make Marco wear the blindfold?'

'I find that depriving him of sight sharpens his other senses. And it is so deliciously tantalising for him to hear what is going on around him, but not be able to see.' Marsha pulled April into a close embrace and pressed her lips into the valley between her breasts. Her mouth left a perfect scarlet imprint on the ivory white flesh. 'You want him, don't you, April?'

'Marco . . . why should I . . .?'

'You want him. I saw the way you looked at him when he brought you to me. Relax, April. There's nothing wrong with liking boys as well as girls. Why deprive yourself of dessert when you can have the whole damn banquet?'

April crossed the room to where Marco was crouching. Marsha was right, and that made her angry. What was happening to her lately? She'd always been adventurous, but right now she hardly recognised herself.

'He *is* beautiful,' she murmured.

'You can have him. You can have me too.'

Marco gazed up with sightless eyes, his lips moist, his smooth, muscular body gleaming with a thin sheen of oil.

'Why don't you say something to him, April? He'll do anything you tell him to. You're his mistress.'

April's mouth was dry. She tried to swallow but there was a lump in her throat and when at last she managed to speak her voice sounded husky.

123

'Stand up, Marco.'

It was an indescribable feeling, giving a man commands and watching him carry them out without question. He got to his feet in silent obedience.

'Take off your leather apron.'

'Yes, mistress.'

Marco reached behind him and unfastened the apron, dropping it onto the carpet at his feet. Underneath he was wearing the briefest of thongs, made from some kind of black cotton jersey which was stretched so thin that the fat, curling snake of his penis was clearly visible. It was impressively large, even in repose, and April wondered how much more beautiful it would be when it was swollen and hard between her fingers . . .

'Do you find me pleasing, Mistress April?'

Marsha cut in, her voice sharp and her nails sharper still as they raked across Marco's cheek. He did not even flinch at his punishment.

'You will *not* speak unless you are questioned. Is that quite clear?'

'Quite clear, Mistress Marsha.'

It excited April in the strangest way to see Marco's wounded face, the four parallel tracks dragged across his skin, at first livid white but turning rapidly to scarlet ridges sprinkled with fine beads of blood. She smoothed the flat of her hand over his shoulder and down his chest, taking hold of his nipple rings and twisting them quite hard.

'Do you enjoy pain, Marco?'

'Yes, Mistress April.'

STRANGERS IN THE NIGHT

Marsha took April's hand and nodded towards the far wall of the room.

'In the cabinet,' she whispered. 'You will find everything you need.'

The cabinet's sleek japanned exterior gave no clue to its contents. Inside were half the contents of a torture chamber: handcuffs, rods, whips, chains, gags, lashes with deceptively soft thongs of chamois leather, tipped with tiny balls of lead shot.

She selected a cane. It was springy and alive in her hand. She could feel its eagerness trembling through it.

'Turn round, slave.'

Marco did so, turning his beautiful smooth back to her. The long, unbroken sweep of back and buttocks begged for kisses, but April burned now with a different desire. It was as though all the rage and frustration she had felt over the past weeks had become concentrated and mutated into a delicious and perverse desire.

The cane fell once, twice, a third time, cutting through the air with a soft swish and striking the smooth, muscled back with a sharp slap. April could hardly control the feelings inside her. Her nipples tingled, her belly ached, her pussy softly contracted and dilated like the yearning mouth of some deepwater anemone. With each stroke, each stripe marking that smooth flesh as hers, her excitement grew. As the blows came faster and harder, her breathing quickened. Marsha's hands were on her, stroking her buttocks, caressing her flanks; her voice whispering beautiful obscenities into her ear.

She could take no more. The pulsing throb of need

Aurelia Clifford

between her thighs was too intense, and Marsha's fingers were creeping closer and closer to the hub of her pleasure.

She threw down the cane. Marco had not flinched once during his punishment, but his shoulders were rising and falling with the effort of controlling his breathing. His back was scored with red welts, and sweat was trickling down into the little hollow at the base of his spine.

'Take off the rest of your clothes and then turn round and face me.'

'Yes, Mistress April.'

Marco's long, tanned fingers hooked under the side strings of the thong and eased it down over his slim hips, stooping to step out of it and lay it on the ground. He turned round slowly.

'You are a filthy minded slave, Marco. Allowing yourself to become sexually aroused without my permission.'

'I'm sorry, Mistress April.'

The tanned serpent had awoken and uncurled itself into a long, hard rod of flesh which thrust out at forty five degrees above shaven and oiled testicles as appetising as smooth skinned fruit. What a strange game this was, thought April – and yet so seductive. Who would have thought that mere dominance could be so sexually exciting?

'Sorry is not enough. I ought to punish you.'

She watched the blindfolded slave carefully, saw how his cock twitched and stiffened at the thought of yet more punishment, yet more pain.

'But that would only give you pleasure,' cut in Marsha.

STRANGERS IN THE NIGHT

'Instead, slave, you shall give pleasure to Mistress April.'

'As you wish, mistress.' His voice trembled.

Marsha's hands were on April's backside, stripping down the rubber shorts and the fishnet tights beneath, baring hips and backside, pulling the pants down almost to the top of her boots.

'Marsha . . .'

A soft voice soothed her, softer caresses smoothing over her bare backside.

'You may lick out Mistress April, slave. But make sure you do it *very* thoroughly, or Mistress Marsha will ensure that you are never capable of feeling pleasure again.'

About the same time that April's sex was discovering the softness of Marco's tongue, Kieran Harte was discovering the unpleasantness of 'helping the police with their enquiries'.

There were two detectives in the interview room, just like on TV, but unlike TV tecs they didn't play Good Cop and Bad Cop. Obviously those two had gone on holiday, leaving Bastard Cop and Sadistic Cop in charge of the police station.

Detective Constable Kline pulled up a chair and sat astride it, his chin resting on the back and his eyes boring into Kieran's.

'What were you doing at Mr Harlesson's house?'

'I've told you!'

'Tell me again.'

'We were colleagues. I was worried about him.'

'Why?'

127

'He had problems – drink mainly.'

'We didn't find any alcohol near the body. The cause of death appears to have been strangulation.'

'If you say so. Look, can I go now?'

Detective Sergeant Baxter responded with a sharp cuff to the side of the head.

'You'll go when I say you can go.'

Hand to his head, Kieran swore under his breath.

'You can't do this! I have a right to speak to a lawyer.'

'Later. How long had you known the deceased?'

'Just over a year. Since I came to work at Mersey Roar. Look, has Graham been told about what's happened? He and Sven . . .'

'Yes. We know. It's being taken care of. Close, were you – you and Sven? I mean, Graham was away a lot, Sven must have got lonely sometimes . . .'

'Not really, I hardly . . . hang on, what are you saying? If it's what I think you're saying you're on completely the wrong track. I'm not gay.'

DC Kline smirked. 'Sergeant Baxter never said you were. Your words, *Mr* Harte. Perhaps there's something you'd like to tell us about your relationship with Mr Harlesson? Bit stormy, was it? Liked to play sex games and they got a bit out of hand . . .?'

Kieran felt a horrible coldness in the pit of his stomach. A few seconds later, he felt a punch in the solar plexus that damn near knocked all the breath out of him.

'Bloody hell . . . what was that for?'

'Just to let you know we've got your number, Kieran, so don't go making any plans for long holidays abroad, will

STRANGERS IN THE NIGHT

you?' Baxter turned to Kline. 'OK, you can let him go now.'

Kieran blinked through eyes blurred by sweat. He could smell the rank scent of his own fear.

'I can . . .?'

'Like I said, you can go. But we'll be watching you, Kieran. Don't pull any stunts because, believe me, we're always one step ahead of scum like you.'

The moment she saw Dan Lauren with Soraya, April knew he *meant* her to see them together. Why else had he chosen to turn up at Mersey Roar at the precise moment when he knew April would be at work on the running order for that night's show?

She stepped out of her office to find them in the corridor outside, ostensibly waiting for the lift. Dan's arm was on Soraya's backside and she was nibbling his neck. They moved apart when they saw April, but without any great sense of urgency.

'April! I . . .'

At least Soraya had the decency to look embarrassed, apologetic even. But not *that* apologetic. Soraya was young and attractive and ambitious too.

'You're all dressed up tonight,' observed April coolly. 'Going somewhere nice?'

Dan threw Soraya a look that spelled b-e-d then offered April a sparkling smile.

'Soraya and I are going out to dinner.' Patting her on the bottom he nodded to her. 'You go on ahead – take the stairs. I'll be right behind you.'

129

'I bet you will,' muttered April, watching Soraya walk down the stairs towards the lobby.

'Not *jealous* are you, April?'

'Should I be?'

'Not as far as I can see. I mean, what's sauce for the goose is sauce for the gander, isn't that right?'

There was something about the look in Dan's eyes that made April shiver – not just with anger or jealousy or lust. The cold hand of unease lay heavy on her skin. He *knew*. That was what all this was about. He was trying to punish her – but for what? How much did he know? About Kieran? About Marsha?

About both?

'I don't know what you're talking about.' She knew she ought to feel guilty, but angry was all she felt.

'Is that so? I thought you'd be the first to understand the principles of natural justice. Repay like for like, that's how it goes. It all seems perfectly fair to me. Besides.' He smirked in a way which was both menacing and unpleasant. 'I don't know what you've got against *women.*'

The lift announced itself with a bright ping and a jolt of machinery. April faced up to Dan, eye to eye. A kind of jubilant anger gave her the illusion of being perfectly in control.

'Fancy a *ride*, Dan?'

Without waiting for his reply, she pressed the button and the lift doors opened. She stepped inside.

'Well?'

Flattered that his shock tactics had had the desired

STRANGERS IN THE NIGHT

effect, Dan stepped into the lift and closed the doors behind him.

'Going to make this worth my while, April?'

Oh, she was going to do that all right. She was going to screw him until he thought he'd died and gone to Heaven. And at the very moment when he thought he'd won, she'd turn round and tell him exactly how it was between them.

'Don't fool yourself, Dan. That's not how much I want you. That's how much *you* need *me*.'

Chapter 8

Time was ticking down towards zero.

It had reached Day seventy nine by the time April next visited Kieran in his flat. She found him hunched over a double espresso, his hair dishevelled and a darkening bruise on his cheek.

'Kieran . . . is something wrong?'

'You could say that.' He forced a jokey smile. 'Out before nightfall again? You want to be careful you don't melt.'

April walked across to the coffee machine.

'Mind if I join you?'

'Help yourself.'

She sat down on one of Kieran's enormous floor cushions, and patted the empty space next to her.

'This is much more comfortable than those horrible kitchen chairs.'

Kieran flopped down beside her.

'I suppose you want me to tell you what's been going on? Are you sure you want to know?'

'I want to know what's making you so miserable.'

Aurelia Clifford

'It's Sven. The police seem to think I did it.'

'You? Kill Sven Harlesson? That's ludicrous! Why on earth would you . . .?'

'You tell me. They've had me in for questioning three times now, roughed me up a little to soften me up, even tried to make out I was having a homosexual relationship with Sven. I don't understand it.'

'It's ridiculous.'

'Yeah? Well you may know that, April, and I certainly do, but as far as HM Constabulary are concerned I'm public enemy number one. Somebody's been telling them lies about me. Hell, I'm almost starting to believe them myself.'

April closed her eyes and leaned back. Everything was spinning inside her head, colours and lights like fragments from a mad kaleidoscope.

'This is a bad dream,' she murmured. 'Why can't I wake up?'

Kieran slid softly down onto his side on the cushions.

'You're tense.'

'Are you surprised?'

'Let's just say I'm not going to let you stay that way.'

Kieran eased off her shoes, sliding his hands up April's legs and unhooking her stockings from their suspenders.

'What are you . . .?'

He stopped her mouth with a kiss.

'You argue too much. Lie back, try to relax. This is going to make you feel good.'

With only the faintest murmur of protest, April sank down until she lay on her back on the pile of cushions. It

STRANGERS IN THE NIGHT

felt like being the pampered favourite in a Sultan's harem.

Kieran began massaging her feet, using firm but gentle circular movements that began just under the big toe and spread out to cover the whole of the foot. He ran his tongue up the sole of her right foot, from heel to the base of the toes.

'Nice?'

'Mmm, Kieran, where did you learn to do this?'

'Let's just say I once had a very interesting relationship with a reflexologist. Did you know that every zone of the foot corresponds to another part of the body?'

'Fascinating.' Despite everything, April was beginning to let go of tension. 'This feels just like . . .'

'Like what?'

'Like floating . . . in warm water. I feel weightless.'

'And how about this?'

Kieran's hands moved a fraction to the right and the feeling changed again. Now April was wriggling like a snake, her whole body suddenly energised.

'What are you doing to me?'

'I'm stimulating one of the pleasure centres. It encourages your body to produce natural endorphins.' Kieran bent down over April's feet and began licking her toes. 'I understand it makes some people feel incredibly sexy.'

In the dark silence of her mind, April was daydreaming. It was a seductive fantasy. It could almost be Marco who was stroking and licking her feet. Sweet, subservient Marco . . .

She thought of the pretty slaveboy, blindfolded and

bare cocked, his tiny thong discarded and his cock dancing and jerking with the sheer pleasure of doing his Mistress April's bidding. How arousing it had been to be in complete control, to bring him to orgasm with just the sound of her voice, as his wicked tongue pushed in and out of her oh so willing pussy.

Only it wasn't Marco she was commanding – it was Kieran. Kieran lying on his belly at her feet, naked and helpless. There was a thick, heavy chain about his neck and she was using it to pull his head down towards her bare feet.

'Kiss them, slave.'

'As you command . . . mistress.'

His lips framed the word so delightfully. She would make him say it again.

'Lick my feet clean, slave.'

'Yes, mistress.'

The very thought of Kieran worshipping her almost made her come. Her body was an aching mass of sensations, centred on the tingling, burning, throbbing hub of her sex.

Domination was not the end of it. She could use her power to hurt him, too. She remembered the black, curling bullwhip in the cabinet at Marsha's house. It had felt so intoxicatingly potent in her hand, flexible and venomous as a spitting cobra. It would leave a thick, red stripe across Kieran's back and he would weep with joy and gratitude. But first she would seize him by the hair, forcing him to bend low and kiss the instrument of his torture.

STRANGERS IN THE NIGHT

'April . . . April, what's got into you?'

Kieran's voice cut into her thoughts, breaking the spell. Where was she, what was she doing? She looked down at Kieran and saw that he was staring at her, trying to free twists of his sandy hair from her clawed hands.

'Kieran . . . oh Kieran, did I hurt you . . .?' She sprang away, suddenly realising that her fantasy had very nearly become reality. 'I'm sorry, I didn't mean to.'

'The massage must be even more powerful than I realised,' joked Kieran, darting kisses on April's bare legs as he slid up her thighs. There was an edge to his voice, and all at once April felt ashamed.

'I'm not . . . I'm not Marsha,' she murmured as though she needed to convince herself. 'I'm *not*.' Kieran looked at her quizzically.

'Marsha Fox? What's she got to do with anything? Have you found something out?'

'No, nothing. Nothing at all.' April slid her hands round Kieran's neck. This time her command was a tender one. 'Kiss me.'

He covered her with his body and then rolled over and over on the cushions, softness and hardness blending as excitement took them over and they began undressing each other. Spilt coffee was sticky and wet underneath them but they noticed nothing beyond the sticky warmth of each other's body.

'You are. The *most*. Sexy woman. In the whole world.' Kieran's words were punctuated by kisses, running over each new inch of April's flesh that he exposed.

She growled and tore off his shirt, paying no heed to

Aurelia Clifford

the sound of ripped cotton or the buttons that flew off as she pulled it down over his arms, baring his smooth chest.

Her teeth bit delightedly into the sweat-seasoned flesh. His nipple was nut hard on her tongue and she flicked the tip over and over it, teasing it as her fingers pinched his other nipple, so hard that he winced and swore with the tender violence of it.

'Bitch,' he cursed, rolling onto his back and pulling her on top of him. His jeans were round his thighs and his body was hard and eager between April's thighs.

'Beast,' she spat back, tossing her head and laughing as Kieran pulled her black stretch minidress down to her waist. Her breasts sprang out, the distended nipples clearly visible through the seamless cups of her moulded bra.

Reaching round behind her, she released the catch of her bra and, bending forwards, let it fall softly away from her breasts. The very tips of her nipples brushed Kieran's chest as she bent low over him, letting them trace invisible erotic patterns on his flesh.

He twisted her hair into a long rope and used it to hold her fast, her breasts pushed hard against his chest, her belly against his belly, her bare legs straddling his hips. He kissed her hungrily as his fingers slid under the short, scrunched-up skirt of her dress and discovered – to his great delight – that April hadn't bothered wearing any underwear.

'Slut,' he murmured, his fingers clenching and unclenching on the soft white flesh of April's backside.

STRANGERS IN THE NIGHT

'My own incredible slut. Do you know what I want you to do to me? Can you guess . . .?'

She answered him by slipping her hand between their bodies. Kieran's dick lay flat against his belly, the tip glazed with a wet ooze of lubricant which smeared her fingers as she took it in her hand.

'Is *this* what you want me to do?' she breathed as she pushed the tip of his cock between her thighs, easing it into the groove between her outer labia, using it to tease the swollen stamen of her clitoris.

Kieran moaned as she tormented him, using his desire to give herself pleasure, masturbating herself with the hypersensitive dome of his glans. He was so desperately close to coming but she was holding him on the edge, bringing herself to the same crisis point so that, when she climaxed, she would make them come together.

Suddenly he felt her bearing down on him. Very, very slowly; more slowly than he could stand. He took her by the hips and hunger overwhelmed him, making him use his own strength to take her. She shuddered and cried out as he pulled her down hard on his dick, impaling her with the force of his need.

The pleasure they shared in those few incredible moments was enough to make them forget that tomorrow they might have only seventy eight days left.

The local media could be vigorous – even vicious – once it scented a big story. And by local standards, the Sven Harlesson scandal was big news. So was the news of Marsha Fox's 'voluntary' suspension.

139

The *Courier* celebrated its good luck by embroidering the facts a little: LOCAL RADIO DJ AND GAY PORNO RING; DID HARLESSON KNOW TOO MUCH?; RADIO BOSS QUITS IN SEX STORM.

Local hero Daniel Lauren, multimillionaire supremo of Viper Sounds, seemed quite surprised to step out of Mersey Roar's front lobby into a forest of microphones.

'Any comment, Mr Lauren?'

'What do you think about the Harlesson case?'

'Who killed Sven?'

'What about the sex allegations? Do you think Marsha Fox is involved? Is that why she quit . . .?'

Dan put up his hands against the barrage of questions.

'Ladies . . . gentlemen, please . . .'

Another microphone was jammed in his face. Someone had turned up from regional news with a TV camera and a sound man.

'About Marsha Fox, Mr Lauren – you know her?'

'Naturally. She and I are *business* acquaintances.'

'And you think she's done the right thing over the Harlesson scandal?'

'Well . . . that's hardly for me to say. But this temporary suspension seems a sensible move, given her position of responsibility . . .'

Mike Meen emerged into the daylight with a smile on his face and a shine on his new leather jacket. Suddenly all the attention switched from Dan Lauren and onto him.

'Over here, Mike – Mike Meen, is it true that Marsha

STRANGERS IN THE NIGHT

Fox has been suspended and you're been appointed station manager?'

Mike shrugged modestly. He had been practising.

'*Acting* station manager,' he stressed. 'And I must emphasise that there is absolutely no suggestion of impropriety. The directors simply felt it was best if someone else took over the daily running of the station while this regrettable spotlight is on Marsha . . .'

April jabbed the remote control at the TV, switching it off. Kieran almost choked on his glass of red wine.

'Bloody hell,' he muttered. 'You, me, Sven, Marsha – who's going to be next?'

'Yeah.' April thought of the look on Marsha's face as she'd told her that she was 'voluntarily' suspending herself until further notice. 'The question is, did Marsha jump – or was she pushed?'

As it turned out, it wasn't so much who was next, as what. Big changes were happening at Mersey Roar. With Marsha suspended and Sven out of the picture, April had to admit that changes were inevitable. She just wished that they didn't affect her quite so much.

It was like a weird game of musical chairs, only in this game there were more chairs than people. Mike had it all worked out. The evening rock show was going to be taken over by Soraya, Sven's drivetime by April, and 'Strangers in the Night' by a bemused kid straight out of hospital radio. Nobody – with the exception of Mike Meen – was even slightly happy.

As for Mike, he was behaving like a triple rollover

141

winner in the National Lottery. He grinned and issued soundbites twenty four hours a day, assuring everybody that it was "only temporary" and that "Marsha would be back in the hot seat very soon", with his fingers crossed behind his back.

'Afternoon tea with April Sanchez'; could things get any worse? Even the name of the show sounded like a heap of crap. She accosted Mike one afternoon in Reception.

'Mike – we have to talk.'

'Sorry, April, you know how it is – things to do, people to see.'

'Don't give me that shit, Mike. What the hell do you think you're doing, giving my show to that spotty adolescent?'

'Julian comes highly recommended. Besides, who's listening at that time of night? We need you on the afternoon shift, April.' He put his arm round her shoulders and she almost fainted from the overpowering smell of aftershave. 'We need your skills and your experience.'

'I'm a rock jock, Mike – an alternative DJ. I don't *do* knitting patterns and recipes. Are you trying to kill off my career for good or something?'

'Of course not, you should see this as a promotion. Proof of my complete confidence in you.'

'That night time show means a lot to me, Mike, I've built it up from nothing. The kid's going to wreck it . . .'

Mike patted her on the shoulder dismissively. His brain was already three quarters of the way to somewhere else and somebody much more important.

STRANGERS IN THE NIGHT

'Catch you later, April. Good luck with the first show! I just know you're going to do a terrific job.'

April watched Mike saunter out through the lobby and climb into the company BMW that had been Marsha's until a couple of days ago. She almost screamed 'I resign' at his retreating back – but what good would that do? Only a quitter would give up now.

The first week of programmes were a nightmare. She hadn't realised just how bad Sven's show really was, or how much his listeners seemed to *like* it that way. Senior citizens, bored housewives and lobotomy patients seemed to make up three quarters of his audience.

Still, the 'phones were buzzing, just like they were on 'Strangers in the Night', only now people weren't calling to whisper their dark secrets or pass on sexy messages to their lovers.

'Play Bing Crosby for me, will you April?'

'That recipe you gave, for Shepherd's pie . . .'

'I've lost my budgie, he's called Horace . . .'

'Will you tell listeners there's a jumble sale at Litherland Church Hall on Saturday . . .?'

Much more of this and she'd go as crazy as they were. And there was so much to cram into the two hour slot: interviews, 'nature notes', wall to wall muzak, 'public service announcements', adverts for anoraks and Volvos, 'Recipe of the Day' . . .

By Wednesday she was operating on automatic pilot. So what if she got the 'celebrity' interviewees mixed up and asked the gardening expert for his views on crocheted balaclavas? It wasn't as if anybody seemed to notice.

143

Aurelia Clifford

'. . . that was *Cherry Pink and Apple Blossom White* by Eddie Calvert. Don't forget our Doc Spot after the local weather. And now it's coming up to four fifteen and it's time for Traffic Report with the gorgeous Stefan Brooks . . .'

She switched off the mike and took a long swig of very thick, very black coffee. It was one way to keep awake. On the other side of the glass screen Stefan was shuffling his papers and going on about a jack-knifed lorry and trailer on the M6. April made a mental calculation. One minute twenty of Stefan, then straight into three Beatles tracks.

Just as she was cueing up the CDs something strange happened. Stefan's voice cut out. She looked through the screen into the next studio. His mouth was still moving and the red light was on, but she couldn't hear a single word of what he was saying. Bloody antiquated equipment, they couldn't even afford a headset that worked.

'April . . .'

'What?'

It was a man's voice, but it wasn't Stefan's. It was coming through on her headset, husky, soft, chillingly familiar.

'You haven't forgotten me, have you?'

Her heart missed a beat.

How could she possibly forget that voice? The voice that had whispered across the night, telling her about the photograph in her studio, the CD on the console that she hadn't even known was there?

STRANGERS IN THE NIGHT

'What do you want?'

'We miss you, April. What Mike Meen did was wrong, taking you away from "Strangers in the Night". We don't want to lose you, we want you back.

'April, come back to us before it's too late.'

Chapter 9

Marsha wasn't surprised by Dan Lauren's arrogance. After all, didn't she know him better than anyone else?

She smiled as she saw that he hadn't changed the locks. Careless, Dan, she thought to herself as she reached into her pocket for the keys he had once given her. They turned soundlessly in the lock and she pushed open the door and walked in.

The black framed mirror in the hallway caught a snapshot of her walking past: a tall figure dressed from head to toe in matt black rubber, tight as a second skin. The rubber mask encased her head completely, leaving only savage slashes for eyes, nose and mouth. Her waist was cinched insect-tight with an elasticated belt which emphasised the roundness of hips and backside. Inside the zip fronted catsuit her whole body was compressed and compacted, her talc-sprinkled skin held in a tight embrace which forced her flattened nipples hard against the seamed inner surface.

Marsha's rubber clad thighs brushed together with a light, whispering swish as she carried her attaché case

Aurelia Clifford

down the corridor towards the living room. Dan's living room.

Her heart beat a little faster and she savoured the slight but pleasurable discomfort of fear. It quickly left her. She was no longer human. She was Nemesis, the spirit of revenge made flesh. This time Dan had gone too far, and no matter what risks she had to take, she would make him pay.

Nothing had changed from the last time she had seen the apartment. Even the arrangement of red roses was identical; preserved in formalin, freeze dried, repigmented to look fresh and alive, they could not and would not decay. Dan Lauren had no time for fresh flowers; they were too disposable and fragile, too demanding. Like people.

It was all as she remembered it. Japanese porcelain, Majolica ware, a Jeff Coons table in the form of a naked woman, bent backwards to balance crablike on fingertips and toes. A Stratocaster, Emulator synthesiser and Dan's collection of blues 78s. Marsha knew exactly where everything was: after all, it had once been hers.

Stepping through the door into the bedroom, she threw the attaché case down onto the bed and began to search the room. Her elbow length black rubber gloves would ensure that she left no prints.

As she opened the door of Dan's mirror fronted wardrobe, she remembered how things had been when they were together. The very first time Dan had brought her here, she had known that he was dangerous. No doubt that was what had first interested her in him, persuading

148

STRANGERS IN THE NIGHT

her that they were kindred spirits. He was unpredictable, unreliable, mercurial, selfish, breathtakingly ambitious . . . She remembered their first time, in this very room. Even as he was undressing her he was telling her that he didn't need her.

'You have to understand, Marsha. I don't need you.' He kissed her neck as he pushed her down on the bed. Mirrors on the wardrobe doors, on the ceiling, reflected the gesture a dozen times. 'I don't need anyone.'

That was enough to make him irresistible – perhaps he had known it all along. Marsha had decided that she would make him need her, would force him to his knees screaming for mercy and then, if she felt like it, she would walk away. Only things hadn't quite worked out the way she'd planned . . .

One wintry night, they had made love on the balcony of Dan's flat, overlooking the river. It had been Marsha's idea, a crazy impulse to throw off her clothes and run out into the freezing darkness.

The night wind lashed her hair against her face and neck as she leant forward over the balcony rail. The balcony was crisp with frost and a light fall of snow beneath her feet, the cold so intense that at first she perceived it as scalding heat. The metal rail was sticky with cold, almost burning her as she leant her belly against it.

Dan was behind her, fully dressed, his hands absurdly hot on her frozen skin. He didn't speak. She remembered the howl of the wind and the husky growl of his breathing, quickening in her ear. Somewhere a very long way beneath

Aurelia Clifford

her, she saw lights moving on the river.

As the snow began to fall, she took Dan's dick in her hand and guided it between her arse cheeks. She shrieked like a she cat on heat as its burning tip entered her, sliding deep inside her, opening her wide. Her lovesong was savage and venomous.

'Bastard, bastard, I hate you, I despise you . . .'

Each thrust forced her so hard across the rail that it bit into the soft flesh beneath her ribs, pushing all the breath out of her. She didn't need to breathe, only to feel the power and the pleasure. He was hers now, lost in the breathless rush towards orgasm. If she had wanted to, she could have thrown herself forward and they would both have plummeted down through the frosty air with the wind screaming in their ears. Perhaps it would have been better if she had simply pushed him over and watched him fall . . .

She closed the wardrobe and began searching through the dressing table, the chest of drawers, even the bookshelves; taking each book from the shelf, shaking it and carefully replacing it in exactly the same position. She would find out everything about Dan, every little secret, and no one would know she had been here.

Marsha glanced at the book in her hand. *Venus in Furs*. She and Dan had read it to each other, experiencing every nuance, living the book. Marsha had taught Dan the pleasure of pain; although astoundingly virile, he had been surprisingly limited in his understanding of sado-masochistic rituals.

She recalled him kneeling on bare floorboards in a

STRANGERS IN THE NIGHT

derelict dockside warehouse, his wrists bound to his ankles with silk scarves and his eyes full of hunger.

The whip curled between her fingers, its tip supple and hungry. It wanted to taste Dan Lauren's flesh and so did she.

'Are you going to whip me?' he had asked her, his eyes full of a dark brightness.

'That depends.' Her high heels tiptapped on the wooden floor, striking up tiny clouds of dust. She circled him, stroking his face and bare torso with the tip of the bull-whip. 'Do you want me to?'

The brief silence was a lot more eloquent than his reply. 'I might.'

She took hold of the chain about his neck and twisted it a little, just hard enough to make his breath rasp in his throat. The hot candlewax had cooled and congealed into scarlet teardrops on his shaven chest; they looked just like a martyr's blood.

'Say "please".'

He shook his head. This game was a new one to him. Dan Lauren had never asked for anything in his life; whatever he wanted he simply reached out and took.

'Untie me, Marsha.'

She laughed and ground her stiletto heel into the soft, upturned sole of his foot. He cursed her, and the warmth of sensual excitement flooded her swollen sex. That night, and that night only, she had had Dan completely in her power.

'You're the slave, Dan, remember that. Your place is to answer and obey your mistress, not to ask her questions.'

151

The wolf's fur stole slipped from her shoulders and she wound it softly about Dan's throat. Its glassy eyes and gaping mouth looked as if it was laughing. She felt Dan shiver at the touch of fur on bare skin. Tiny beads of perspiration were forming into trickles which dripped down into the small of his back.

'Untie me.'

'I will untie you when both of us are good and ready.' She lifted her right hand and the bullwhip rolled down into a long, fat snake of polished hide, its tip slithering in the dust. 'For now, I think it is high time I taught you the price of insolence.'

Even now, if she closed her eyes, she could smell the tang of his sweat, and feel the spurt of his semen onto the shiny toes of her boots. Dan had been an apt pupil. It was a pity that he had never learned to control his need for power over everything and everybody. And after what had happened to Sven Harlesson . . .

Marsha turned back to the attaché case on the bed. She snapped it open with gloved fingers. Everything she needed was here. When April found these things in Dan's apartment she would know that Marsha Fox had been right.

And then April Sanchez would know who she could trust.

Day sixty five brought the customary card to April's doormat. By now she had become accustomed to them, scarcely glancing at them before putting them away in a drawer of her kitchen table.

STRANGERS IN THE NIGHT

But this card was different. There was a printed message inside:

**GIVE OUR REGARDS TO SVEN, APRIL.
YOU'LL BE SEEING HIM SOON.**

Hands trembling, she stared at the words, not really seeing them, only hearing them inside her head like some macabre echo. She scarcely remembered seizing her car keys from the dresser, jumping into her car and driving the few miles across the city to Dan Lauren's flat.

'Dan.' Her fists hammered on the door. 'Dan, for God's sake open this door.'

Everything was quiet. Perhaps he wasn't in, she should have called him first. She shivered. Why had she come here anyway? She wasn't sure. Because she knew him? Yeah. Maybe also because she knew that she could trust him.

Dan found April huddled against the doorframe, shaking.

'April – what the hell? Are you okay?'

Strong arms dragged her into the flat, closed the door, sat her down in a deep, soft armchair.

'What's happened to you, April?'

She reached into her coat pocket and handed over the card.

'This came. Today. Dan, somebody wants to kill me.'

He read the message, shook his head, threw the card into the wastepaper bin.

'Dan . . . don't!'

'That's what you should do with all of these. They're

153

just a sick joke, you shouldn't take them so seriously.'

He was surprisingly tender. His strength was warm and all consuming, and April snuggled into it like a baby bird into a nest. He handed her a glass.

'Here, drink this.'

'What . . .?'

'Brandy. It'll make you feel better.'

She grimaced.

'I hate brandy.'

'You'll like this one. Besides, it's medicine.'

He perched on the arm of the chair and guided the glass to her lips. April was surprised to find that he was right. The liquid was slightly warm, soft tasting and grapey, with a hint of something spicy that she didn't quite recognise.

'There's something in it?'

'Just something to relax you. Herbs and spices, my own recipe. Finished?'

She nodded, feeling like a child as Dan scooped her up in his arms and carried her across the room, through the door and into the bedroom, laying her down gently on the bedspread.

'Roll onto your belly and relax. I'm going to give you a massage.'

The brandy had gone straight to April's head. She felt floaty and slightly lightheaded, maybe a little silly too. All the darkness seemed to be drifting away, leaving her feeling warm and relaxed and maybe a little aroused.

Dan undressed her quickly, easing off her shirt and jeans. She felt the soft ping of her bra catch, then the

STRANGERS IN THE NIGHT

elastic sliding sharply across her back. He slid his hands underneath her body and pulled it away from her breasts, linging long enough to cup them in his hands and squeeze them rhythmically between his fingers.

'Mmm . . . nice.'

'Good. Good . . . just relax. Leave everything to me.'

His fingers hooked under the elastic sides of her cotton briefs and slipped them down over her hips. April raised her belly a fraction off the bed to help him pull them over her backside and thighs.

'Now, just lie still. I'll be back in a moment.'

She scarcely noticed how long he was gone. Somewhere to the right of her she could hear the tinkling of glass on glass, but it seemed not to mean anything very much. She was warm, happy, unafraid. Dan had been right. There wasn't anything to worry about, not as long as she had Dan Lauren to take care of her.

When he returned, he was carrying a small blue glass bottle.

'Special massage oil,' he explained. 'I've warmed it to release the active ingredients, it should feel good.'

How good, April could not have imagined. Dan took the stopper from the bottle and poured some of the oil directly onto her back. It felt gloriously warm, like bottled sunshine, and where it trickled and oozed it seemed to awake tingling, trembling sensations which made her whole body quiver with excitement.

He began working the oil into her skin, using his fingertips to brush it lightly across the surface. She sighed and let her body sink into the soft bedcover, occasionally

155

arching her back or pushing out her backside to receive his caresses.

'Wherever did you learn to do this, Dan?'

'There's a lot I can do to make you feel good.'

He kneaded the tension from her shoulders, bathing her in warm fragrance, smoothing the knots from her muscles as he worked his way slowly down to her shoulderblades, her ribs, the small of her back.

'You have a fantastic backside, did I ever tell you that?'

April felt as though she was shimmering with sensual electricity, radiating a special heat that came from the very core of her sex. She was softly pulsing to her own secret rhythm. Dan's fingers were smoothing warm, spicy oil over her backside, making it run in viscous trickles into the deep cleft between her buttocks, to pool in the hidden eye of her anus. She wanted him, hungered for him, had to have him.

She rolled onto her back, and smiled up at him through drowsy eyes, mouthing the first words that came into her hazy, fuddled brain.

'Fuck me.'

Dan slid on top of her, fully clothed, taking her feet and placing them on his shoulders so that her thighs were spread wide apart and her backside was lifted off the bed, revealing the deep red gash of her sex.

His fingers slid down the deep, wet gully.

'Is *this* what you want?'

April gasped her appreciation.

'Yes.'

'And *this*?' His index finger scored a tight circle about

STRANGERS IN THE NIGHT

the exposed button of her clitoris, pulling down its fleshy hood and forcing it to pout its unashamed desire.

'Yes, yes, yes!'

Her fingernails became claws, digging into Dan's waist through his linen shirt and dragging him down on top of her. But he made her wait, teasing her with his fingers until the juice dripped out of her and made a wet stain on the bedspread beneath her.

'Tell me how much you want it.'

'Please . . .'

'How much, April?' The fingertip teased even closer to the painfully swollen crest of her clit.

'*This* much.' Taking his other hand, she guided it between her thighs and into the deep, well-oiled crease between her buttocks. Her anus was alternately contracting and dilating, aching with the need to be filled.

He slid into her in a long, slow stroke which seemed to go on for ever. His dick was in her arse and the fingers of his right hand were sliding and twisting inside her vulva, pushing insistently deep inside her. Suddenly she wanted more and more.

'Fist me, Dan. Do it, please.'

She moaned with extreme pleasure as she felt his fingers curl into a fist and slide smoothly into her, stretching the walls of her sex, forcing inside her until they were pushing against the neck of her womb. Strange how she had never wanted him to possess her so completely before. Perhaps she needed the security of his possession . . .

It was afterwards, as they sat in the jacuzzi together, that Dan put a treacherous thought into her mind.

157

'Frankly I'm surprised you came to me, April.'

'Surprised? Why?'

Dan lay back and let the jets of water pummel his body.

'Surely your *good friend* Kieran has been getting these cards too?'

It was only then that it dawned on April. No. No, Kieran hadn't. And why might that be?

'Are you trying to feed those ducks or kill them?'

April was standing by the lake in the park, aiming lumps of stale bread at the water with such force that they disappeared beneath the surface. She swung round and offered Kieran a scowl.

'What's it to you?' Throwing the last of the crumbs onto the ground, she screwed up the plastic carrier bag and dropped it into a nearby litter bin.

'You've been avoiding me.'

'That's rubbish.'

'I don't think so.'

April set off across the park. Kieran watched her for a couple of seconds, then set off in hot pursuit, catching up with her within a few long strides. He touched her shoulder but she shrugged him off.

'Leave me alone.'

'You might at least tell me what I'm supposed to have done.'

This time she stopped abruptly and didn't push him away. She half turned towards him.

'Nothing.'

'Then why the cold shoulder?'

STRANGERS IN THE NIGHT

'Things are getting scary, Kieran. Cards, messages, I can't trust anyone.'

'Even me?'

'Especially you.' She walked on a few yards further. He stopped her with a hand on her elbow.

'What the hell is that supposed to mean?'

'Only that I keep asking myself why I'm the one who gets all the cards and messages and weird 'phone calls. What's happened to you, Kieran?'

He stared at her in baffled frustration.

'You're telling me you can't trust me just because we're not getting his 'n' hers death threats?'

'Don't be so bloody facetious, Kieran, you know exactly what I mean. Don't you think it's a bit odd that bad things keep happening to other people – me, Sven, even Marsha – but you keep coming up smelling of roses?'

Kieran felt like thumping his forehead against a tree trunk.

'For God's sake, April, I found Sven Harlesson's body, I had a going over by the police, or have you forgotten that? Because I certainly haven't.'

'Oh yes. Sven. That was very convenient, wasn't it?'

'What do you mean?'

'The police thought it was all rather convenient too, didn't they, you just happening to be passing when Sven was lying dead in his own bed?' April wished she hadn't spoken even before the words were out of her mouth. 'Look, Kieran, I . . .'

He swung April round and as she raised her hand to pull herself free, their gazes locked.

159

Aurelia Clifford

Kieran saw it in a flash of realisation. The fire . . . it was still there between them, they couldn't deny it, no matter how much they might want to. They were made for each other.

'You can trust me, April, I swear you can.'

'If only I could be sure of that.'

She looked at him long and hard; then, gently detaching herself from his grasp, she turned and walked on down the path.

Alone in her flat that night, April turned on the radio.

She hadn't meant to. In fact, she had told herself that she definitely wouldn't. 'Strangers in the Night' belonged to someone else now, to that beardless adolescent Julian Prince . . .

Jealous anger gnawed at her guts. It hadn't been a good day, she'd hated every second of the afternoon shift and it had showed. She'd tried going to bed but she couldn't sleep. All she did was lie there staring at the hands on the clock ticking round past midnight, imagining what she'd be saying if she was sitting in the studio right now.

Pouring herself a hot drink, she curled up in a chair next to the radio and clicked it on. She didn't want to listen but it had become a life or death compulsion.

Fifteen minutes of pap were enough and she found herself in her car, foot on the floor, driving hell for leather through the empty city streets towards Mersey Roar.

As she burst into Studio 2, some middle aged bore was telling the world how brown rice had changed his life. It was more than April could stand.

STRANGERS IN THE NIGHT

'For God's sake, Julian, this isn't late night entertainment, this is medicine for insomniacs.'

Hastily, Julian clicked off the mike and went to the next record. 'What the . . .?'

'Get out of the way, Julian, this is my show and I'm taking it back.'

'You can't do this!'

'I can, and I am.'

Three minutes and twenty three seconds later, it was April Sanchez whose voice greeted listeners to 'Strangers in the Night', April's fingers that curled about the stem of a microphone as though it were a lover's dick.

'Welcome to the darkness, night owls, the Queen of Night is back to swallow your souls. Invoke me and I'll materialise from your radio to make you feel good . . . and very, very bad. Call me.'

She ejected *My Way* from the CD player, rummaged through a pile of tat and emerged with *Bedtime Story*. Not great maybe, but the best of a bad bunch.

Julian Prince watched with growing fascination from the corner.

'You're insane.'

'You say the nicest things.'

'You think you can get away with this?'

She smiled at him and licked her lips. 'Darling, I'm certain I can. Give me half an hour and you'll see what I can do with this show.'

As the track ended the 'phone lines were a mass of wildly flashing lights.

'Caller line one. What's on your mind?'

161

Aurelia Clifford

'Welcome back, April.'

That voice. *The* voice, the voice of all her nightmares and her fantasies. She felt hot, cold, dizzy, suddenly afraid. She had to force herself to sound . . . normal.

'Hello, caller. Wanna talk?'

'You know what I want to do to you, April?'

She paused, but the words forced themselves between her lips.

'Why don't you tell me?'

'I have this pair of solid silver handcuffs, they're so beautiful, I had them made especially for you. And a pair of cuffs for your ankles, too, lined with fur. I'm going to chain your wrists to the bedhead and your legs wide, wide apart. And then I'm going to lick out your pussy and fist you in the arse, all night long . . .'

April was mesmerised by the low, husky voice. Julian was hopping about behind her, cursing and trying to shut down the mike, but she pushed him away. She was fixated, she had to know . . .

'Want to hear more, April?'

'Tell me. Tell me it all.'

'I want to take you to the zoo and put you in a cage, April. My beautiful she cat. I want a thousand people to watch you masturbate – you'd like that, wouldn't you, April. *Wouldn't you?*'

She longed to scream yes, yes, yes, but all that came out was a husky whisper.

'Is there more?'

'There's always more, April. Always more for you. How would you like me to take that microphone and push it

162

STRANGERS IN THE NIGHT

right up inside you? How would like me to strip you naked and fuck you in the snow? How would you like me to come to your apartment and make Kieran Harte watch you getting it on with me . . .?'

She listened in stunned silence, her heart pounding, her head spinning. How could she admit how much these dirty minded fantasies were exciting her?

'I . . .'

'You *would* like that, wouldn't you, April?'

At last she found her voice. It was a slick voice, seductive yet distant.

'Well thank you, caller, and now let's go to line two . . .'

But the voice wasn't going to let go of her quite so easily. It pursued her relentlessly, telling her truths that she simply didn't want to hear.

'I've missed you, April. We all have.'

'But not as much as you've missed us.'

Chapter 10

'Do we *have* to go?'

'Of course.' Dan slipped on his grey Armani jacket and brushed a few hairs off the sleeve. ' "Battle of the Bands" is an important sponsorship deal for Viper Sounds. I have to show my face at the semis.'

April put down her lipstick and looked over her shoulder at Dan.

'You do realise most of the bands are rubbish? There's hardly an ounce of talent between them.'

Dan allowed a faint smile to twist the corners of his cruelly sensual mouth.

'Talent isn't what you need to succeed in today's music business. I'd have thought you of all people would realise that.' His hand rested lightly on the swell of her buttock. 'You look great in leather. It brings out the animal in me.'

April finished painting on a perfect crimson pout, glossed her shaggy black curls with a little styling serum, and straightened up. She blew Dan a kiss in the mirror.

'We don't have to go anywhere tonight. We could stay right here.'

Aurelia Clifford

'Don't tempt me.' Dan checked his watch and drew away. 'The car will be waiting for us downstairs. I told Robinson to bring it round for seven thirty.'

'The play-offs *start* at seven-thirty. We'll be walking in halfway through the first band.'

Dan laughed drily.

'What better way to get noticed?'

The second semi-final of 'Battle of the Bands' was being held in a recently renovated 'community theatre' on the outskirts of the city centre. As she walked in April could still smell the cloying heaviness of slow drying gloss paint.

Some teenage girlie duo were squeaking and gyrating on the stage as they pushed their way through the crowd and took their seats in the empty raised section at the back. Short sleeved white angora sweaters that hugged adolescent breasts and bared several inches of tanned midriff, pink satin microskirts, shiny wetlook boots and frilly white lace knickers; these girls might sing out of tune, but you couldn't ignore them.

'Who's the jailbait?' demanded April.

'They call themselves Funbundle. The tall girl's sixteen, the blonde one's only fourteen – great tits, don't you think?'

'You're a filthy old pervert, Dan Lauren.'

'Yeah, well, dirty old men buy records too. Maybe these kids will get themselves a contract with Viper Sounds even if they don't win the contest.'

'They can't sing, they can't dance . . .'

'But put their hair in pigtails and give them lollipops to

166

STRANGERS IN THE NIGHT

suck, and perverts all over the north west will be coming in their pants.' Dan slid his hand sideways onto April's knee. 'Speaking of which, I want you, April Sanchez. I want you right now.'

'Dan . . .'

'I want to push up that horny leather skirt and fuck you.'

April felt her cheeks burn crimson.

'Someone will see.'

'Who? We're alone back here, everyone's far more interested in what's going on on the stage. And besides, who cares if they want to watch?' Dan's fingers pinched April's nipple, making her shudder with unwilling pleasure. 'Haven't you ever done it with an audience before, April? You surprise me.'

He pulled her towards him and they kissed. April's hunger for him surprised her. Her tongue pushed greedily between his lips and she tasted the delicious aroma of him, the mingled flavours of black sugared coffee and Calvados, the scent of musky cologne and showered skin, cool and still moist.

As they embraced, Dan took her hand and guided it to his lap. He didn't need to tell her what was on his mind. His beautiful cock was an iron spike between his thighs, arching up towards his belly. She traced its outline with her fingertips, felt it move jerkily at her touch and grow even stiffer.

She emerged breathless from the kiss. Her tongue lapped the salt from Dan's cheek, skirting up the side of his face and throat to discover the soft lobe of his ear.

167

Aurelia Clifford

Even above the thump and whine of the music, her whisper throbbed into his brain.

'I want you too, Dan Lauren. I want you inside me. Now. But how can we . . .?'

'Sit on my lap.'

Dan's strong hands took her round her waist and dragged her onto his knees. He teased the back of her neck with kisses and lovebites that would have to be very carefully camouflaged in the morning.

One hand remained on April's waist, innocently holding her steady as he kissed the side of her throat. To any casual observer they were just a bloke and his girl, necking as they watched the show. But Dan's right hand was already sneaking underneath April's backside, sliding between grey cashmere and black leather to discover the paradise within.

April shivered with guilty excitement. It she was caught having sex in public with Dan Lauren, she might as well wave goodbye to what was left of her career; yet the fear of discovery only served to heighten her arousal. Right now all she wanted was to feel the burning spear of his manhood pushing inside her, filling her up, satisfying the itch to fuck.

Tonight she was wearing stockings and suspenders. She'd known when she chose them that they would turn Dan on – had she secretly anticipated what was happening now? Dan's fingers slid under her short skirt and discovered the inches of bare flesh between stocking tops and briefs. He toyed with the waxed smoothness of her skin, squeezing and caressing her thighs before moving towards her buttocks.

STRANGERS IN THE NIGHT

The tiny thong barely covered her modesty, and the thin string which held it in place at the back disappeared into invisibility in the deep valley between her buttocks. Dan amused himself by tracing its progress down from the dimple at the small of her back, along the secret pathway which led from her anus to the moist haven of her sex.

'My, my, April. What a naughty girl you are.'

The game was a favourite one. He was the teacher and she was the naughty schoolgirl, the teenage nymphet who seduced her master into arcs of delicious depravity.

'Am I?' she purred.

'Your knickers are all wet through, you wicked girl. You've made a damp stain on my best trousers. You know, I think I shall have to punish you for that.'

'Dan. Oh Dan . . .'

His index finger wriggled about underneath her and pushed aside the crotch of her thong, baring the ill concealed secret of her hunger. With a swift movement of his right hand, Dan had unzipped himself and the finger was replaced by something much thicker, harder, more merciless. Instinctively she raised her hips an inch or two above Dan's lap, and he positioned the tip of his manhood at the entrance to her sex.

He slid both hands onto her hips and pushed her down hard on the upraised spike of his penis. It was all April could do not to curse and moan with the savage excitement of it.

The first rending violence of Dan's penetration was followed by long, smooth, lubricated strokes so slow and

169

controlled that only the most eagle-eyed observer could have guessed what was going on. It was so strange to be making love with Dan and all the time watching the show on the stage. Funbundle were followed by Omo, Omo by a band April found curiously familiar, though she was sure she'd never seen them before . . .

VanillaSex . . . they were good, *really* good. Sexy as hell, good looking boys too – one hundred per cent gay, of course, in an arousingly menacing kind of way. There was something incredibly horny about that lead singer, posturing in those cutaway PVC bondage pants that exposed the perfect moons of his deliciously firm buttocks. There was a Bowie knife through his belt and one of the backing singers was kneeling at his feet, simulating oral sex with the blade . . .

As the lead singer's powerful voice soared above the chugging rhythm of guitars and drums April couldn't help thinking she'd seen this seven piece somewhere before . . . but *where*?

Pretty soon the effort of thinking coherently was too much to cope with. Dan's hands were vice tight on her thighs, controlling the rise and fall of her pussy sheath about his dick. She wanted to go harder and faster and more and more frantic, but that wasn't what Dan wanted. And Dan, it seemed, knew everything about April's pleasure, even more than she knew herself. He knew that slower meant better, and longer, and more intense.

April was caught in an unreal world. Dan was making love to her, but it was the gay boy on the stage who mesmerised her, his oiled torso crisscrossed with buckled

STRANGERS IN THE NIGHT

straps and the bulge of his cock ominously swollen beneath the crotch of those too tight pants.

Was it crazy to want him? She imagined that she was the guy kneeling at his feet, mouth open to offer a perilous tribute to the knife blade. Or on her hands and knees, her skirt pushed up and her bare arse spread wide to receive ten inches of swollen cock, sheathed in studded rubber . . .

Where had she seen him before? Did it matter? Not now, perhaps not ever. All that mattered was Dan's hot seed, spurting into her, and the orgasm that was rising up her like a scalding tide, taking her over and drowning her in the sea of her own ecstasy.

On her next day off, April took a trip down to London to shop for clothes. The clothes were just an excuse really; getting away was what it was all about, getting away from Mersey Roar and reminding herself that ordinary people were getting on with their ordinary lives all around her.

She'd heard about an exclusive new arcade which had opened up near Victoria Station, featuring the work of up and coming British fashion and jewellery designers. That would be her first stop; then lunch at Harvey Nichols, followed by a few designer sales and finally the train back to Liverpool.

The arcade was hidden behind a row of three-storey eighteenth century houses and was almost invisible from outside. Beyond the gates, it opened into a vast domed courtyard roofed with glass, with a fountain and ornamental trees at the centre.

She strolled around the various shopfronts. Most of the

clothes on display were disappointing: too conventional or too expensive, or both. Then her eye was caught by a smaller unit almost hidden behind a cappucino stall. Brightly coloured trousers and skirts in Kevlar, PVC and rubber; dresses in leather and linen. Fun fur, see-through plastic and Neoprene. This was much more promising.

The girl behind the counter was reading a copy of American *Vogue*.

'Can I help you?'

'I'd like to try a few things on. Do you carry a full size range?'

'Reasonably full, but anything we don't have we can make to order and deliver within seven days.'

April browsed along the rails, selected an armful of dresses and trousers and walked through to the row of changing cubicles at the back of the shop.

She undressed quickly and checked the price tag on a purple fur and linen jacket. Three figures, pricey but affordable if it looked good. She tried not to think that in a couple of months' time she might be out of a job.

Or worse . . .

The jacket didn't look right on her. It was too short in the arms, too loose about the bust. But the sleek sleeveless minidress in broad horizontal bands of white PVC and black Neoprene fitted her like a second skin, the tight fabric and excellent cut making the most of her breasts and the scoop neckline offering tantalising glimpses of a generous cleavage she hadn't even realised she had.

She was just admiring her rear view in the cheval mirror when she heard it. The voice from 'Strangers in the Night'.

STRANGERS IN THE NIGHT

'Hello, April.'

An icy hand seemed to descend on her bare shoulders, turning her smooth skin to gooseflesh. She swung round, shocked and trembling.

'W-what . . .?'

'You should know by now, you can't trust anyone.'

It was coming from the next cubicle. Not bothering to change, not even bothering to pick up her purse or her credit card wallet, April tore aside the curtain and rushed out, pushing open the curtain of the next cubicle.

'Not even yourself.'

She stood staring into it, transfixed.

It was empty, save for a cassette player on the floor . . . and the pictures. There were dozens of them; no, hundreds, plastered all over the walls of the cubicle, floor to ceiling. Polaroids with one important thing in common: Dan Lauren was in every single one.

She scanned them slowly, incredulously, not quite taking it in yet. They were colour snapshots, garish and explicit. Pornographic, even. This one here . . . she touched it with her fingertip, half expecting it to evaporate at the touch. It showed Dan on his knees behind a well endowed blonde, giving it to her doggy style on a green and gold Chinese rug. April knew that rug. It was in the living room of Dan's apartment. The girl was pneumatic and over made up, her lips pouting and her eyes tight shut. Dan was pulling her head back with a long leather dog leash, attached to a heavy studded collar about her neck.

The next showed Dan in cowboy style leather chaps, his

173

dick emerging from between them and onto the tongue tip of a blindfolded girl with small, pierced breasts. His arm was lifted behind his right shoulder, about to bring down a riding crop onto her bare back.

More. There were so many more, dozens and dozens, and April didn't want to see any of them. Pictures of Dan tying women up and beating them. Pictures of him fucking smooth round arses and huge, swollen breasts in the shower, on his bed, over his desk. Pictures of him masturbating them with dildoes, sucking them off, fisting them, making them answer his need for gratification.

Doing all the things he had done with April Sanchez; and much, much more.

On the floor beside the cassette player lay a photograph album. April picked it up with trembling hands and opened it. It contained more pictures of Dan with his lovers, only this time each lover had a double-page spread of twenty polaroids to herself. A double page, and then no more. Right in the centre of the book she found what she had been dreading: twenty garish pictures of herself with Dan, and her name carefully inscribed underneath in gold ink. The pages were full. It was all so very logical, so very final.

Someone had been watching. Cold shivers turned her skin to goosebumps. All the time she'd been with Dan, somebody had been watching. Taking photographs. Getting off on her pleasure . . .

Against her instincts, she turned the page. This first page of the double spread was scarcely half full; evidently

STRANGERS IN THE NIGHT

this particular liaison was a new one, one which hadn't yet run its course . . .

She took one look at Soraya's immaculately made up face, her painted lips closing around Dan's dick, and flung the album to the floor. An envelope fluttered out and she bent to pick it up. Inside she found a typewritten message:

STILL THINK YOU'RE SOMETHING SPECIAL, APRIL SANCHEZ? TIME TO THINK AGAIN.

Dan was pleasantly surprised by April's eagerness.

All evening at the restaurant she'd been coming on strong to him, showing off her body in that new PVC sheath dress she'd brought back from London, practically offering herself to him with every spoonful of crême brûlée she fed him from her own silver spoon.

He licked the sugary crystals from his lips. They were sharp, like tiny, needle fine shards of glass.

'You're a prick tease,' he commented.

'Not at all,' she countered in that low, soft voice she used on the radio, and which never failed to rouse Dan's sexual interest. 'I'm a woman who knows what she wants.'

'And what you want . . .?'

'Is another glass of champagne. And you.'

April took the bottle of Veuve Cliquot from the ice bucket and divided the remaining contents between her glass and Dan's. It was their second bottle, and she'd been careful to make sure that Dan had drunk most of it. That way, he would be more . . . malleable.

Dan drained his glass and clicked his fingers. A waiter

glided out of the shadows with a notebook and pen.

'Sir? Madam?'

'The bill.' Dan reached into his wallet, took out a ten pound note and stuffed it into the waiter's top pocket. 'You will hurry it up, won't you?'

'At once, sir.'

'Money talks,' he observed, taking out his gold Amex card and throwing it onto the snowy tablecloth.

'So does sex,' replied April, sipping her glass of champagne. She needed to keep a clear head.

The bill duly arrived and Dan signed the credit card slip with a flourish of his Schaeffer fountain pen.

'Your coats, sir?'

'At once. And hail us a taxi.' He looked across at April, her bright pink nails tapping lightly on the outside of her champagne flute. 'Your place or mine? Or would you rather book a room here for the night?'

'Yours. Of course. Hotel rooms are so impersonal. Besides . . . think of all our toys at your place. We could play such interesting games.'

She took her coat but didn't put it on. She wanted Dan to have the full benefit of the dress she had bought at the arcade. White PVC and black Neoprene blended with surprising but absolute sexiness, moulding her body into a perfect hourglass shape, small at the waist, generously round and firm at bust and arse. Her hair was piled up into a sexy cascade of curls, and her long, smooth neck was set off by long black and white earrings designed to look like dominoes.

The taxi was waiting at the front door of the hotel.

STRANGERS IN THE NIGHT

'Where to, mate?'

'Corbridge House.'

The taxi driver surveyed the couple. The bloke was slightly pissed and looked loaded, and he resolved to double the usual fare. The girl – well, she looked sort of familiar. Sexy too. Small wonder they couldn't keep their hands off each other. He grinned as he watched them in his rear view mirror.

'Sure you two can wait till we get there?'

All the way back to Dan's place, April played it hard and sexy. In point of fact she actually felt sexy, but in a savage and unforgiving way. She clawed at Dan's clothes and kissed and bit him, and he responded by pulling her head down towards his lap.

She sucked his cock a little, but only a little. She wanted to drive him crazy, not satisfy him. By the time they got out of the lift and walked down the corridor towards Dan's apartment, they were all over each other, ripping off bits of each other's clothing and dropping them where they fell, kissing and clawing and biting like wild animals.

'Got to have you, got to have you,' he murmured, jerking down April's zip and pulling her dress down over her breasts. It slithered to the floor and she stepped out of it.

'You're mine tonight.' She slid her hand down the front of Dan's trousers and caressed the long, hard pole of his manhood. 'You have to do everything I want you to.'

This game was a familiar one to Dan. He enjoyed it – on a strictly occasional basis of course; you couldn't make a habit of letting your lovers dominate you. But there was a certain sense of liberation in letting go, abandoning all responsibility for your pleasure to a woman who knew how to take ten seconds of pleasure and turn them into an hour.

He was slightly drunk. He hadn't realised it until the cold night air hit him outside the restaurant, but he'd definitely had one glass of champagne too many and was feeling agreeably warm and confused. For once in his life he was happy to let April take the lead.

'Want you . . .' he muttered. She had hold of his arm and was dragging him into the bedroom.

'Come with me. You're mine, remember? You're my slave and you have to do as I say.'

'Oh yes . . . your slave.' He heard himself laugh. It was a good joke, the idea that he could ever be April's slave.

The bed seemed to leap up to meet him and he lay there for many moments, half on his side half on his back, watching the ceiling slowly rotate above him.

It was the jingle of the chain that made him turn towards April. She was carrying an armful of things, things he didn't know that she knew he had. Come to think of it, he wasn't even sure he recognised all of them. How had she found those things?

'Where . . .?' he began, but the words stopped in his throat.

'Lie still, slave.'

She smiled at him and slipped the ropes around his ankles, tying them fast to the posts at the bottom of the bed. He felt instantly even more aroused. They had played this game a few times, but he had never felt quite such enthusiasm for it as he did right now. The ropes were

STRANGERS IN THE NIGHT

rough and tight about his ankles, and when she bound his wrists to the bedposts and slipped a chain about his neck, he began to understand that this time, the rules of the game might have changed a little.

A sudden surge of panic sobered him up enough to realise that this time he really was helpless. He tried pulling against the ropes, but they were knotted fast and there was no way he could make his hand small enough to slide it out through the noose. What was more, the harder he pulled, the tighter the ropes became. They hurt too, abrading his skin until it stung and burned.

'April . . . if this is some kind of joke . . .'

Walking away, April opened her evening purse and took something out.

'April . . . loosen these ropes.'

She did not reply, but walked back towards him. He saw that there was something in her hand.

'OK, so you're a sexy bitch, April. You've made your point . . . now untie me.'

Instead, she climbed onto the bed and knelt on his chest. He could hardly breathe and what air he did manage to drag into his lungs was full of the perfume of her sex.

'Recognise *this*, Dan?'

She pushed the first of the photographs into his face. It showed a man fucking a blonde girl doggy style, while he pulled hard on a dog leash which encircled her slender neck. He struggled to bring the image into focus.

'April . . . who? Where did you get that?'

It was only when she slipped the choke chain about his

179

Aurelia Clifford

neck and jerked it really tight that he began to understand what all this was about. Even as he was clawing at the chain and gasping for breath, his cock was swelling to agonising stiffness.

At last she slackened the chain. He had hardly three seconds to get his breath back before she was thrusting a second photograph at him, then a third and a fourth. Each was more explicit than the last, offering glimpses into a secret world of unusual pleasures which, until now, Dan Lauren had been keeping very much to himself.

'And this, Dan? And this? How many women have you had, Dan? A thousand? Ten thousand?'

With each new photograph came a new and exquisite torture, acting out the image in the snapshot; and after each new punishment, she held the picture over his face, tearing it with relish into many tiny fragments. Dan realised that he had underestimated April Sanchez. Certainly he had never imagined she possessed quite such a subtle skill with sensual torture.

The fifth picture showed him lashing a girl's bare backside with a silver handled riding crop. And here April was, inexplicably with the very same riding crop in her hand, bringing it down with well directed strokes onto his belly and thighs. How his cock ached and tingled as the tip of the crop kissed his balls, making him gasp and curse with humiliating pleasure.

'Bitch. Bitch, horny bitch . . .'

'How about this picture, Dan? Does it bring back happy memories? Was she better than me?'

'Aaah . . .'

180

STRANGERS IN THE NIGHT

'Did you enjoy flaunting it, Dan? Did you get a kick from trying to humiliate me like I'm humiliating you now? What does it all mean?'

Sweat was trickling down from his scalp. He had to shake it out of his eyes to focus on the photograph. It showed Soraya in a fetish harness, a weird confection of shiny red straps that buckled tight about her body and between her legs, forcing into relief her breasts, her buttocks and her pussy lips. He was standing beside her, tightening the straps, making her throw back her head and scream for the pleasure of the pain.

April had a harness in her hand; a shiny red thing made not for a woman but for a man. She buckled it about Dan's dick and balls and he cried out as the straps tightened. The pain was constant and intense, almost but not quite enough to bring him to the most incredible orgasm he had ever experienced. To his astonishment he realised that the wetness on his cheeks was not sweat but tears.

'April . . .'

'What's that, Dan? You want to come? You want me to make you come?'

'Yes . . .'

She laughed as she knelt over his face, masturbating herself to a climax that she would not allow him to share. When she came it was alone, allowing him only the small comfort of her honeyjuice, trickling like warm sweet rain onto his parched lips.

Satisfied, she got off the bed and got dressed. Dan followed her with the eyes of a hunted animal. Suddenly the stakes had risen and he wasn't sure he wanted to be in this sex game any more.

'April. April, what the hell do you think you're doing?'

'I'm leaving.'

'You can't do that. Untie me now.' His wrists strained at the ropes which bound them, but all they did was cut deeper into the flesh. 'Come here and untie me, you stupid little slut.'

April picked up her coat and rested her hand on the door handle.

'I may be a slut, Dan, but I'm special. *Really* special. You have to understand that. It's me or no one.'

And with that she walked away, leaving a very puzzled Dan Lauren wondering what the hell April Sanchez might do next.

Late that night, April drove up to the front of Marsha Fox's house. The lights were still on and when she rang the doorbell Marco answered, suave and darkly beautiful in his tuxedo and black tie.

'Good evening, Mistress April.'

'Is Marsha in?'

He inclined his head respectfully as he answered in his soft Italian brogue.

'I will inform her that you are here. If you would care to come in and wait . . .'

A spark of interest passed between them. There was a yearning gleam in Marco's eyes and April knew what he wanted from her, what he expected from her as his mistress. She would not disappoint him. In any case, her anger

STRANGERS IN THE NIGHT

against Dan Lauren was still fresh enough to be directed at any man who happened to get in her way. Pushing Marco aside roughly, she forced her way past him into the hallway.

'I am not accustomed to waiting. You will take me to Mistress Marsha immediately.'

'But . . .'

She struck him across the side of his beautiful olive skinned face with the back of her hand. The place where she had hit him blushed magenta and she felt a sudden desire to kiss his hurts better . . .

'*Immediately*, Marco.'

'At once, mistress.'

He led her upstairs, past Marsha's collection of early English porcelain and a collection of Eastern rugs, used as wall hangings. Marco hesitated outside a door at the end of the corridor, then knocked.

'Mistress Marsha?'

'I have told you before, Marco, I am not to be disturbed when I am in the bath.'

'Mistress Marsha . . . I am sorry. But . . .'

'But what, imbecile?'

April cut in, as impatient with Marco as Marsha obviously was.

'It's me, Marsha. April Sanchez.'

Marsha's response was a long, soft sigh of pleasure.

'April. April, what a pleasant surprise. Bring her in at once, Marco.'

Marsha was reclining in pale green, scented water in a round sunken bath with goldplated taps. Her dark hair

183

was wet and combed back from her high cheekboned face, making her look at once exotic and regal. April couldn't quite decide if her smile was welcoming or triumphant.

'You look tired, April. Won't you joint me?'

April looked down at the water. It did look inviting – warm and tranquil, scented with a scattering of fresh herbs and lemon grass to relax and invigorate.

'Well, I . . .'

'Undress Mistress April, Marco.'

'At once, mistress.'

All April's vestiges of reluctance faded away at Marco's respectful touch. He knew exactly how to undress a woman: softly and efficiently, letting the clothes caress her body as they sank down under their own weight. But it was not Marco she was looking at; it was Marsha.

Marsha's eyes never left April's body as Marco undressed her.

'You're very beautiful, April.' Her voice was caressing and seductive. She reached out her hand. 'Join me, April.'

April stepped down into the bath. The waters were warm and inviting, but not nearly as welcoming as the touch of Marsha's hands on her tired and naked body. April felt herself relax in Marsha's embrace. For so long she had held back, wary of everyone.

But now she was beginning to believe that at least Marsha Fox wouldn't betray her.

Chapter 11

'I wouldn't want to outstay my welcome.'

April was sitting on the edge of Marsha's brass bedstead, stretching out her right leg and pointing her toe so that Marco could roll down her stocking. Marsha was kneeling on the bed behind her, kneading the tightness from her shoulders.

'Stay as long as you like.'

'You mean that?'

Marsha traced the path of her fingertips with a line of kisses which stretched from one shoulder across to the other.

'April darling, you know I love *having* you.'

As she spoke, she let her hands slide slowly down from April's shoulders to her breasts, their pink muzzles clearly visible through the white satin camiknicker. April raised her hands to cover Marsha's, showing them how she liked to be pleasured, with broad circular movements that rubbed the satin across the crests of her nipples.

In the few days that she had been staying at Marsha's

185

house, April had settled in remarkably easily. It felt surprisingly natural to share a bed – and a bodyslave – with another woman, and it was that very naturalness that made April feel vaguely uneasy. Was this all too simple, too unthinkingly pleasurable? Was she turning her back on her problems and trying to pretend that they didn't exist? Not to mention turning her back on Kieran . . .

'Maybe just a few more days then . . . but I must go back.'

'Why?' Marsha encircled April with her arms and drew down her head into her lap, stroking the hair back from her cheek. 'You could sell the flat, move in here with me permanently.'

'I . . . couldn't.' You could, whispered a voice in April's head. You could sell up, run away, bolt the doors and lose yourself in pleasure.

'Think about it. There's no pressure. Take a few days away somewhere if you need time to think. I'll still be here when you've made up your mind.'

There was a calm certainty in Marsha's caresses, and it occurred to April that for Marsha at least, there were no doubts. April would move in; she and Marsha and Marco would become the ultimate sensual ménage-à-trois. If the thought hadn't been so seductive, perhaps it wouldn't have frightened April so much.

Marsha clicked her fingers and Marco was at her heels like a well trained gundog, his smooth oiled nakedness emphasised by the tiniest of white g-strings.

'Mistress Marsha?'

'Bring a towel and some warm water. Oh, and some of

STRANGERS IN THE NIGHT

the peppermint massage oil and some unscented talc. Mistress April wishes you to wash her feet. Well, what are you waiting for, I shan't tell you twice!'

She dealt Marco a hearty slap on his retreating backside.

'That boy is pretty, but . . .'

She stroked April's bare arm, easing the strap of the teddy down over her shoulder and stooping over to kiss it. April growled her pleasure and curled into a ball, her face buried deep in Marsha's lap and breathing in the scents of her freshly-showered sex.

'Mmm . . . that feels nice.'

'Then I'll do it some more.' She kissed the bare shoulder again, letting her tongue tease the skin into rippling shivers of appreciation. 'Should I get rid of him, do you think?'

'Who?' murmured April drowsily.

'Marco, of course. Is it time I found him a stricter mistress who will discipline him more thoroughly?'

April laughed softly and stretched out her hand to caress Marsha's backside.

'Stricter than you?'

'*Much* stricter. I'm just a pussycat. Well, what do you think?'

'I think . . . I think he's devoted to you.'

'Naturally.'

'And deliciously beautiful.'

'Of course. You don't think I would select just *any* young man to be my slave? Any more than I would choose just *any* young woman to be my lover . . .'

187

Aurelia Clifford

'And he knows so many ways to make a woman feel good . . .'

Marsha laughed, digging her hand deep into the dark tangle of April's hair and twisting it round so that April was imprisoned somewhere between pain and pure delight.

'I do believe my little Marco excites you. Are you telling me I should be jealous of my own slave?'

'Of course. After all, Marco does have the most appetising dick I've tasted in a long while.'

'More appetising than my pussy?'

April pushed her face down between Marsha's thighs. The brown thicket of pubic hair was still moist from her shower, and released a potent fragrance onto her lips as she kissed it.

'I can't think of *anything* more appetising than this.'

As Marco came back into the bedroom with a soft white towel, china bowl of warm water and bottles on a tray, Marsha parted her thighs slightly, to allow April to lap idly at her pussy.

'We've been invited to a party tonight,' she announced. 'A fancy dress party.'

'We?'

'Well, me actually. But the invitation tells me to bring a guest, and I can't think of anyone I'd prefer to take with me. I've had a costume made for you. I hope you like it.'

April raised her head. Her lips were wet and sticky.

'You knew I'd say yes?'

'I know so much about you. Call it instinct. You may begin, Marco – and make sure you do it properly.'

188

STRANGERS IN THE NIGHT

'Yes, Mistress Marsha.'

April stretched out on the bed, luxuriating in the sheer bliss of having a naked Adonis washing and pampering her feet.

'The water is the correct temperature?' demanded Marsha. She sounded as though she half hoped it wasn't, thought April. There seemed little doubt that Marsha got most of her kicks from vengeance, at least where Marco was concerned.

'Oh yes.'

'You are too indulgent, April. Marco is a clumsy imbecile.'

April felt Marco's fingers massaging the soles of her feet, sliding up her ankles, her calves, patting them dry and smoothing a tingly peppermint lotion all over the skin. On this point at least, Marsha couldn't have been more wrong. She felt a certain mischievous delight in oohing and aahing and sighing, wriggling her toes and making Marsha insanely jealous of the liberties her slave was taking with her lover.

'Mmm . . . this feels like *heaven*.'

Marsha's voice was brusque and commanding.

'Leave us, Marco.'

'Yes, Mistress Marsha.'

April sat up. Marsha was scowling.

'Just when I was beginning to relax . . .'

'The boy was starting to irritate me.'

April chuckled and snuggled close into Marsha's nakedness.

'He's just a slaveboy, Marsha. I was doing it to make

you jealous.' She pressed her lips to Marsha's breast, drawing moist circles about the areola with the tip of her tongue. 'What can I do to make you feel better?'

Marsha ran her finger down the side of April's face and pushed it into her mouth, savouring the fertile warmth of her saliva.

'I'm sure we can think of something,' she murmured, and slid between April's sweat moistened thighs.

The party was a huge media event, held in a former warehouse which had been converted into an entertainment arena with several stages, two dancefloors and a mezzanine floor with a bar and discreet seating booths.

Marsha and April arrived around ten thirty, just as the party was starting to hot up. Even in the pandemonium of three competing live bands, and the bright turmoil of advertising executives and television producers at play, they caused heads to turn. April noted the smile on Marsha's lips and realised that this was exactly how Marsha had planned it. If there was one thing Marsha hated, it was *not* being the centre of attention; that at least was something that April Sanchez could understand.

Marsha swept into the main auditorium with a swish of satin drapery. Her costume suited her personality brilliantly. She was a warrior woman, something between an Amazon huntress and Aphrodite, one breast bared by her short white tunic, her legs slim and brown in leather strapped sandals and a quiver of arrows over one shoulder.

STRANGERS IN THE NIGHT

She was leading April Sanchez on a long golden chain. April the she leopard, the hunting cat prowling on hands and knees through the crowd in a satin touch suit with a long silky tail and pointed ears. Each movement seemed to make the leopard print fabric ripple across her skin, deepening the creases at the top of her thighs, throwing into relief the hard-tipped swell of a breast, the long smooth curve of buttock and thigh.

A man touched his companion on the arm.

'Who *is* that?'

The girl sniffed. 'Some exhibitionist bitch.'

She tried to draw her lover's attention back to herself, but his eyes were fixed on the girl in the leopard suit, his tongue flicking nervously over his parched lips. Nor was he the only one to have noticed. Other voices came to April's ears as she padded behind Marsha, winding her body round the forest of legs, rubbing herself against eight-denier nylon and Italian cut trousers.

'That beautiful arse . . .'

'Wouldn't you just *love* to . . .?'

'. . . my cock between those lips . . .'

The girl had been right, thought April. She *was* an exhibitionist, deep down. It felt incredibly stimulating to display herself like this, to draw the gazes of men and women and feel her power to make them want her.

Hands reached out to stroke her and she arched her back, savouring the long, smooth sweep of a palm running down from the nape of her neck to the curve of her backside. Others, less subtle, made fumbling grabs for her and she turned on them, baring her teeth and hissing,

191

Aurelia Clifford

delighting in the way they sprang back, momentarily disconcerted.

The crowd seethed around her. On her hands and knees April had a very different view of the party to Marsha. While Marsha was talking to people somewhere above her head, April was peeping through the gaps between the guests' legs, catching tantalising glimpses of constantly shifting tableaux.

A couple were having sex on the dancefloor, not ten yards away from her. She watched them, mesmerised and excited. The man was sitting halfway up a short flight of steps and his girl sat facing him, the white spike of his cock clearly visible as she moved up and down on his lap. Shifting coloured lights made it all seem robotic and unreal, like the voices that swam in and out of focus around her.

'. . . Didn't expect to see you here, Marsha.'

'Why's that, Dan? Surely you haven't been avoiding me? Although God knows you've enough reason to.'

'Don't flatter yourself, Marsha.'

A jerk on the chain about her neck brought April back to reality, homing in on a familiar voice. She padded forward into the light. Dan Lauren was talking to Marsha. Dressed as a fin de siècle dandy with tiny red horns emerging from his dark hair, he looked every inch the devil in an Edwardian melodrama.

'I've brought a . . . friend with me.' Marsha signalled to April to come forward. 'Of course you already know April Sanchez, don't you?'

Fixing him with her eyes, daring him to look away, April got to her feet.

STRANGERS IN THE NIGHT

'Hello Dan.'

He flinched visibly at the sight of her.

'You.'

'Yes, Dan. Me. You didn't think I'd gone away?'

'Sorry Marsha, I have to go. I have a meeting in ten minutes.'

Eyebrows raised, Marsha watched Dan push his way through the crowds towards the mezzanine bar. She looked quizzically at April, running her fingers down her back.

'How very strange. Is there something about you and Dan Lauren that I should know?'

No matter where April went, the cards went too. They had reached Day thirty two now, and were turning very mean indeed – not that the police wanted to know. As far as they were concerned, female DJs who made 'provocative' radio shows should expect to receive 'challenging fan mail'. She recalled her latest foray to the local cop shop, taking with her this morning's card.

'What are you going to do about this?'

The desk sergeant glanced at the card and went on writing in the day book.

'Another one?'

'Another one.'

He sighed and folded his arms.

'I've told you, miss. I know this business is unpleasant for you, but look . . . when this joker actually *does* something, come back and tell us. Until then, there's not much we can do . . .'

193

Unpleasant? Sick? She sat on the edge of her bed and stared at today's card. Whoever was sending the cards had decided that it would be a good joke to remove the White Rabbit's head and replace it with April's, and now the threats had become positively crude.

She opened the card and looked at the image inside: a drawing of a girl with tousled black hair, copulating with a skeleton. A *skeleton*. Something clicked at the back of her brain. She'd seen this picture, or something very like it, somewhere before.

And she'd just remembered where.

All of a sudden, things began to click into place. Picking up the telephone receiver, she jabbed out a number and waited. A sleepy voice answered.

'Mmm?'

'Kieran? It's April. Look, I can't explain right now, but I need you to do something for me.'

April had grown to detest working at Mersey Roar. It was only stubbornness that kept her from resigning: or at least, that and the fact that every now and again, Julian let her take the helm of 'Strangers in the Night'.

It was after a particularly horrible afternoon show that she walked out of Studio 3 and bumped straight into Mike Meen in the corridor.

'Hi, April. Everything OK?'

'As a matter of fact, no, it isn't. I want a word with you.'

'I'm busy. I have meetings all afternoon.' He tried to push past, but April barred his way, forcing him into a corner.

STRANGERS IN THE NIGHT

'Now.'

'Look, can't it wait? Make an appointment with my secretary for next week sometime . . .'

'No, it can't.' April was standing only six inches away from him now, invading his personal space and making him feel very, very uncomfortable. 'Tell me something, Mike. Do you like what I'm doing with the afternoon show?'

'Sure I do.'

'You listen to the show then?'

'Of course.'

'So what *exactly* do you like best about it?'

'You're doing a great job, April, but really I do have to go.'

He was astonished by the force with which she slammed him up against the wall.

'April, what the . . .?'

She was right in his face now, smelling the edge of fear in his sweat.

'You don't listen to my show at all, do you Mike? You never have and you don't give a damn what I do with it.'

'That's crap and you know it.'

'Do I Mike? Do I really?'

'I'm acting station manager here, April. It's my *job* to care. My head's on the block if people don't like what we broadcast.'

'Somehow I don't think so. Would you like to know what I *do* think? I think I was taken off the breakfast show because I was making too much of a success of it, and given the graveyard shift to shut me up—'

'Don't be absurd—'

'—and when that took off too, you had me transferred to the afternoon show where you *knew* I'd die of sheer bloody boredom and take the show with me. I think you're deliberately trying to run down this ratio station, Mike, so our franchise is taken away when it comes up for renewal. The big question is, why are you doing it?'

Mike's cheesy smile darkened then switched back on, like a faulty light bulb.

'Like I said, April, you're doing a great job.' With an effort he pushed past her and walked off towards the staircase. 'I want you to know we all have complete confidence in you.'

Yeah, thought April darkly. Complete confidence in my ability to fuck everything up. Should I be flattered, or insulted, or just plain scared?

'Mistress. Oh mistress April . . .'

Marco was enraptured. April, his beautiful stern Mistress April, was drawing the blade of a long kitchen knife lightly along the length of his stiff manhood. A tender warmth flooded him and it took all the self control he could muster not to climax. That, of course, would have been the ultimate transgression and Marco wanted so much to please his Mistress April.

He sighed and opened his eyes as the cold steel blade left his cock and she laid it down on the table. Seconds later he felt her sharpened nails raking down his bare back.

'You will keep perfectly still, slave.'

STRANGERS IN THE NIGHT

'Yes, mistress.'

'You will give no sign of pain or pleasure.'

'As you command, mistress.'

'You will obey me and think only of your mistress's pleasure, never your own.'

He whimpered softly at the cold sharpness of her nails digging deep into his flesh as they slid down over his back and over the hard muscle of his backside. His cock jerked but did not spurt; in the months of training which Mistress Marsha had lavished upon him, he had quickly learned how to control his sexual desires so that he could ejaculate virtually on command.

'Your pleasure *is* my own, Mistress April.'

'That is as it should be.'

She signalled that the test was at an end by slapping his firm young backside.

'You have done well, slave.' The four brim full glasses of water were still sitting squarely on the tray, and Marco had not spilled a drop despite the severe sensual torments he had been subjected to. She stepped away and walked to the other end of the kitchen. 'Now you may let go of the tray.'

Marco released it from his grasp and the glasses fell to the tiled floor at his feet, shattering into sharp fragments.

'Mistress?'

'Walk towards me. Over the glass.'

The fragments were knife sharp but Marco did not hesitate. He welcomed the pain, tears of ecstasy running down his cheeks as he stumbled towards his mistress across the shattered glass.

197

Aurelia Clifford

She was waiting for him with other pleasures, even greater than the last. Embracing him from behind, she took his cock in her hand and began masturbating him.

'You will not climax, Marco. Not yet.'

'No, mistress.'

'You will control yourself until I tell you you may come.'

'Yeeees. Mistress. Oh, mistress . . .'

It was very, very difficult to concentrate his mind on not coming. He focused his thoughts on cold things, on unattractive, repulsive, unsexy things. It wasn't easy. Even with his eyes closed he could see April's moist, pouting lips and feel her hands skilfully stroking his dick.

He was almost grateful when she stopped. At least the agony subsided to an aching throb of need. Mistress April darted a row of kisses up his spine, at last reaching the back of his neck.

'You will answer any question I ask you, Marco?'

'Yes, mistress.'

'Then tell me. Does Mistress Marsha have a special room – a study, perhaps?'

'Yes, mistress.'

'Take me there.'

She felt him tense in her hand.

'I cannot. Forgive me, Mistress . . .'

'Marco, do you wish to displease me?'

'No, Mistress April.'

'Then you will take me there immediately.'

Marco led the way up the back stairs which led out of the kitchen and had once been used by servants to reach

198

STRANGERS IN THE NIGHT

their quarters in the attic. He paused in front of a door on the second floor landing.

'Here, mistress. She keeps it locked.'

'Open it.'

'Mistress, I . . .'

'Open it.'

Marco took the key from where it lay on the top of the doorframe, and unlocked the door. The room behind it was unremarkable in itself – long, thin, scarcely wider than a corridor, with whitewashed walls and a sloping ceiling. It was not the room but its contents which interested April.

'Leave me and wait outside. You will *not* speak of this to Mistress Marsha.'

'No, Mistress April.'

Alone in the room, April took advantage of the opportunity to search it from one end to the other. It contained a variety of ingenious sexual toys – love eggs; spiked butterfly stimulators, huge two-branched dildos, straps and chains and tiny silver clamps designed to be clipped onto the nipples, clitoris or scrotum.

She slid open the drawer of Marsha's bureau and found something else lying inside; something which began to bring everything else into focus.

Another piece of the jigsaw puzzle.

Kieran was still not sure why he was doing what April had asked him to do. Their relationship was to say the least an on-off one. For the last week April had been shacked up with Marsha Fox, and it wasn't as if April had ever really

Aurelia Clifford

ditched Dan Lauren either. So where did that leave Kieran Harte? Confused, frustrated, mad as hell – and desperate to have her back in his bed.

Hands thrust deep in his pockets, he paced up and down uneasily. It was dark here on the Liverpool waterfront at two a.m., and he didn't feel safe. His imagination drew knifemen in the shadows and drowning faces in the ripples on the surface of the river.

'What do you think you're doing here, Kieran Harte?'

Kieran's blood froze in his veins. It was a man's voice and it was right behind him; low, menacing, and curiously familiar. The voice that had spoken to April on 'Strangers in the Night' . . .

He tried to look behind him but the voice barked out a command.

'No. Don't try to turn round, you might regret it. I asked you a question: what are you doing here?'

'Just.' He swallowed. 'Walking.'

This is it, he thought, already picturing the police pulling his sodden corpse out of the Mersey. Any minute now I'll be playing the big celestial disco with Sven Harlesson.

'Do you know why you're here?' The voice was angry, he didn't know why but wished he did.

'No. Should I?'

'I'll ask the questions, Kieran.' The voice paused. He could hear breathing right behind him, so close he thought he could feel it like a hot breeze on the back of his neck. 'Is your cock stiff for me, Kieran?'

'W-what?'

In astonishment, he swung round. A figure in jeans and

STRANGERS IN THE NIGHT

tee shirt was standing right behind him, a little black box thing pressed to its mouth.

'*April?*'

She stepped forward out of the shadows, her arms falling to her side.

'Me.'

'Who was that . . . and where's he gone? How . . .?'

She laid a hand on his arm. The touch felt good and warm.

'I'm sorry if I startled you.'

'Oh don't mention it. You only took about twenty years off my life.'

April smiled. She looked white faced and frail in the moonlight and all of a sudden he wanted to protect her.

'Like I said, I'm sorry. I think I've probably been a bloody fool. Can you forgive me?'

'Not a chance.' But his shameless cock had forgiven her already, and his kisses were not far behind.

Chapter 12

'Feeling warmer now?'

April reached up to turn off the shower and the cascade of hot water turned to a light trickle of warm, fat droplets. Her legs were still wrapped round Kieran's waist and she could feel the cooling rivulets of his semen meandering lazily down her inner thigh. He kissed the end of her nose and lowered her slowly to the tiled floor.

'Exhausted. You're a wicked woman, April Sanchez.'

'Don't tell me – you want me to promise never to change.'

'Not unless it's into a red leather catsuit with zips in all the right places . . .'

Laughing and kissing, they tumbled out of the bathroom and onto April's old pine framed bed. It creaked in protest as they rolled into the centre of the sagging mattress.

'I think we may have broken your bed,' commented Kieran, running his fingers over April's backside and toying with the moist, sensitive entrance to her sex.

'So we'll buy another one. Tell you what, let's burgle a

203

Aurelia Clifford

bed shop and try out all the beds.'

Kieran's finger pushed a little deeper into April's tropical haven.

'Nah. Let's *break* all the beds.'

They made love again, this time with April on top. They moved well together, their bodies enjoying a new and instinctive intimacy which simply hadn't been there before tonight. Afterwards, they curled up together on the duvet, waiting for dawn to come up over the city. April snuggled her head into the crook of Kieran's arm.

'Mmm. We need another shower.'

'I'll lick you clean.' Kieran lifted April's head and ran his tongue tip lightly over her lips, savouring the remembered taste of their lovemaking. How often had he fantasised about having April's lips once more about his dick? And not once had he come close to realising just how good it would feel. 'April . . .'

'Hmmm?'

'How's about you explain just exactly what's been going on? I mean, it's not that I'm complaining or anything, but I don't normally take a stroll along a derelict dock at two o'clock in the morning.'

April lifted her head and darted a trio of kisses on Kieran's nose, lips and chin.

'What do you want to know?'

'You could start by telling me how you did that stunt with your voice.'

'Oh, you mean this.' April rolled over and fished the little black box thing from under the bed. It looked like a pocket dictaphone, with a mouthpiece and a couple of

STRANGERS IN THE NIGHT

silver buttons. 'I found it in Marsha's apartment.'

Kieran took it and turned it over in his hand.

'A voice synthesiser? You mean Marsha was . . .?'

'The mystery male called to "Strangers in the Night"? Yeah. Crazy, huh?'

'But why?'

'That's easy. Marsha has a thing for me . . .'

Kieran grimaced. 'Don't remind me.'

'At first the calls were meant to frighten me and make me dependent on her, so that I'd run to her every time anything went wrong. And so that I'd make mistakes in my job, maybe even crack up. Then Marsha really got into it and it started to turn her on, knowing I was on the other end of the line listening to her fantasising about what she'd like to do to me.'

'So this whole thing is about Marsha's lesbian fantasies?'

'No, there's a lot more to it than that.'

'You think Marsha's behind everything that's happened then – Sven, the cards, the threats?'

'No, none of that. I think she was involved at the beginning, in a plot to finish off Mersey Roar and set up a rival radio station, then she got scared and wanted out when Sven Harlesson was killed. But she knows exactly what's going on and she's been trying to protect me from it.'

'OK. I'll buy that, as far as it goes.' Kieran poured two glasses of red wine from the bottle by the bed. 'But *what* does she know? Who's behind all this, April, and how do we get it to stop?'

205

Aurelia Clifford

April sipped at her glass of wine. It was dark damask red, like crushed rose petals; the colour of Marsha Fox's velvet bedspread.

'Well . . . Marsha's out of the picture at Mersey Roar; either she jumped or she was pushed. Mike Meen's taken over – have you ever asked yourself why?'

Kieran scratched his head. Now that April mentioned it, it did seem odd that a bloke like Mike Meen, who'd been rapidly approaching his radio sell by date, should suddenly be snatched from obscurity and thrust into the limelight.

'He's not exactly Mister Dynamic.'

'He's not even Mister Barely Adequate. When you and I joined the station, his show was way over budget and losing listeners hand over fist. No one in their right mind would put him in charge of the station.'

'But he's certainly enjoying being acting station manager,' pointed out Kieran. 'Not to mention fronting "Battle of the Bands". Obviously he thinks he's doing a great job even if nobody else does.'

'Oh yeah? April pressed her lips against Kieran's, eating him up with wet, winy kisses. 'It hasn't occurred to you that he might actually be deliberately running down the station and the DJs – in fact everything except "Battle of the Bands"?'

'It might look that way,' admitted Kieran. 'If it made any sense.'

'Maybe it does. You know I was at the last semi final with Dan Lauren?'

'Uh-huh. So?'

206

STRANGERS IN THE NIGHT

'So the winners were a band called VanillaSex. A gay kitsch heavy rock outfit, pretty good too. In fact, so good that I realised I'd seen them somewhere before. On the *professional* circuit in London.'

'But "Battle of the Bands" is strictly for amateurs. That's the whole point of the competition.'

'Exactly.' April slid off the bed, walked across to the wardrobe and rummaged about in the blanket cupboard at the top. She brought out a dusty A3 portfolio, tied with faded green ribbon. 'Great. I knew it was still here somewhere.'

Kieran raised an amused eyebrow.

'Don't you ever throw anything out?'

'Only my lovers.' She smiled archly. 'So you'd better watch your step, big boy.' Unfastening the knotted ribbon, she opened up the portfolio. It was crammed with old publicity photographs and posters. 'I kept these from when I was down in London, working as a reviewer on *New Music Now*.' She slid out three black and white promotional stills and laid them on the bed. They showed a seven piece Goth band, all black leather, white painted faces and black lipstick. 'Recognise them?'

Kieran stared at the picture.

'Now you come to mention it . . .'

'They weren't called VanillaSex when this photo was taken, they were called Diabolic Shroud and their whole image was completely different. Oh yeah, and as I recall they used to do a really menacing version of *Run Rabbit Run* as an encore . . .'

Kieran heard the words echoing in his brain. 'Run

207

Kieran Run . . . there's a bullet in your head and you're very very dead . . .' Could this be that same band?

April went on.

'A lot of influential people had a lot of money invested in them, they were going to be the next Mission – only then the bottom dropped out of the Goth market and the investors got their fingers burned. Now look carefully at the backdrop behind them.'

Kieran felt a cold shiver of recognition run down his spine. Behind the lead singer was a huge hoarding with graphics that were all too chillingly familiar. A skeleton, having sex with a Goth chick. The same picture that had been inside the card sent to April . . .

'Hold on, April . . . you're telling me that a one time failed Goth band, a professional band, has entered "Battle of the Bands" under false pretences and is sending us death threats?'

'No, Kieran. Not them.'

'Then who?'

The wine-darkened lips curled into a mischievous smile.

'I shan't tell you if you don't give me a kiss.'

'April . . .'

'Ask me how I know so much about Diabolic Shroud.'

'All right, how?'

'Sven Harlesson told me.'

'*Sven?*'

'He used to be the drummer with Diabolic Shroud. He knew everything, Kieran. In fact, somebody thought he knew too damn much.'

STRANGERS IN THE NIGHT

April *had* to front 'Strangers in the Night', this night of all nights. She was hot and sexy and provocative, and she was going flirty-fishing on the airwaves for the prey she knew was waiting somewhere out there.

Caller Line One was a girl with a sultry, tremulous voice that shimmered with excited desire. She told the world about her latest sexual adventure; how she'd answered an ad in a contact magazine and had gone to her first swapping party. How last night she'd driven out to the Delamere forest and joined a dozen total strangers for unfettered, voyeuristic sex in cars with steamed up windows . . .

By the time the girl rang off, the airwaves were vibrating with sexual tension and April's palms were wet with anticipation. Somewhere out there, a certain person was listening, just waiting for the right moment to call in.

'The thermometer's burning hot, children of the night. Let's see if we can make it melt . . . Now, who do we have on line two?'

'Hello April. Have you missed me?'

The mystery voice was as soft, dark and unmistakably masculine as ever. Strange how real the deception was, even when April knew exactly what was happening.

'Good to talk to you again, caller. What are you going to tell the night owls?'

'You've been a naughty girl, April. You can't get enough of it, can you? You just love having a man's dick in your mouth . . .'

April cut in abruptly.

'Caller, everyone knows that *this* kitty loves to drink

209

cream, but what about you? What about you, caller? What do *you* like?'

The caller did not answer, but the rasp of heavy breathing filled April's headset. She licked the dryness from her lips.

'I know what you like, caller. You like red velvet basques and no knickers. You like girls with bare backsides, bending over your lap. You like beating them until their cheeks turn scarlet and they scream and wriggle. You like wriggling your tongue inside their pussies and licking out the juice . . .'

'April . . .' There was a hint of urgency in the voice now, a note of panic behind the measured, masculine tones. April knew that she was getting through, and she turned the heat right up.

'You'd love to watch two girls getting it on, wouldn't you caller? You'd love to masturbate as you watch them body surfing and licking each other out. You'd love to do it to *me*, wouldn't you, caller? All you really want is to do it to me and have me do it to you . . .'

'April!'

'It's true, isn't it?'

'April, April you bitch! I need you . . .'

April smiled. She had won.

'So does everyone else, Marsha. Everyone needs to be fucked by April Sanchez. Now, who do we have on line three?'

The final of 'Battle of the Bands' was scheduled for the next evening, at the new riverside arena in Liverpool.

STRANGERS IN THE NIGHT

'Dan's certainly pulled out all the stops,' commented Kieran as he and April stepped out of the black limousine and walked up the steps to the front door, accompanied by the click and flash of press cameras.

'Of course he has,' replied April. 'He thinks he's going to pull off the media coup of the decade and get absolutely everything he wants.'

'And is he?'

There was rather more meaning than there might have been in Kieran's voice. April pulled a face.

'What do *you* think?' She gave Kieran a kiss on the cheek. 'Just sit tight in the audience and keep your fingers crossed, okay?'

'You're sure you know what you're doing?'

'No. I'll just have to make it up as I go along.' April glanced around and caught sight of Dan Lauren, having a last minute word with Mike Meen and a lighting technician. 'Look, there's Dan – I'll see you later.'

Catching sight of April, Dan dismissed Mike and the technician with a wave of the hand. He looked edgy, half hostile, half fascinated, thought April. Little wonder he couldn't take his eyes off her. She'd spent hours getting ready for tonight, having her hair smoothed and straightened, squeezing herself into the hired white and gold Versace gown which had been intended for Soraya . . .

'Hello Dan, *darling*.'

Dan's eyes travelled up from April's gold shoes to her stockinged leg, bared to the thigh by the slashed skirt of the gown, past the underwired bodice to the low cut corsage, diamante choker and elbow length white gloves.

211

'April.'

'You don't look very pleased to see me.'

He laughed drily.

'I'm a little . . . surprised, that's all. You're full of surprises, aren't you, April?'

April looked down at the gown.

'Oh, you mean *this*? I have to look good if I'm presenting the award.'

'You're . . .?'

'Didn't they tell you? Soraya couldn't make it. You could say she was unavoidably detained.'

Unavoidably indeed, thought April. Detained by the length of sashcord she and Kieran had used to tie her up. She'd be lying if she said she hadn't enjoyed it.

'I see.'

'You're not . . . disappointed, are you?' She reached out an immaculate gloved hand and stroked her index finger down the front of Dan's trousers. 'I mean, it's not as if I *meant* to hurt you that time at your flat. It's just that I get a little rough when I'm having fun.'

She was good. Very good. So good in fact that she felt the sudden swelling hardness under her fingertip. Dan could play it cool but his libido would always let him down. She smiled and licked her lips.

'I'm really looking forward to working with you tonight.'

Dan caught her hand and carried it to his lips.

'Yeah. Of course. It'll be a pleasure. Maybe afterwards . . .?'

'Why not? If nothing more important comes up.'

STRANGERS IN THE NIGHT

The contest began. April sat with the judges at one side of the stage. There were three of them: Mike Meen, somebody from Viper Sounds and a guy from a music therapy charity which had been promised a fat handout from Dan Lauren. Not what you'd call an impartial jury, but then what did you need impartiality for when the result had already been decided?

Six acts came, played and went. Five of them – including Axehead – were tedious, talentless and very obviously amateurs. The sixth were VanillaSex. The minute they took to the stage it was obvious they were going to win. They were a perfectly manufactured product, with all the expensive equipment, the backing tapes, the designer gear, the horny dance routines . . . and the music. It came as little surprise to anyone when they won by a mile.

April got up on stage with Dan Lauren, to present the award. The band were smiling, the audience stamping their feet, Dan grinning like a well fed alligator as he made the official sponsor's speech.

'. . . Viper Sounds is proud to present this year's award to VanillaSex, the sound of the future. We'll be backing them all the way with a three album record deal and live dates all over Europe and the UK.' He leaned his elbows on the lectern. 'In fact, VanillaSex are just the kind of band I'm looking forward to hearing on my new radio station . . .'

What? The gasp from the audience echoed the jolt inside Kieran's head. A new music radio station . . .?

'. . . yes, ladies and gentlemen, I am pleased to announce that Viper Sounds will be bidding against

Aurelia Clifford

Mersey Roar for the music radio franchise this September. Northern Lights FM will be at the cutting edge of music broadcasting . . .'

Dan was so surprised when April seized the microphone that he didn't even try to stop her cutting in.

'Is that so, Dan? You want to discredit Mersey Roar and then outbid us to win the franchise, is that right? Well before you do that you'll have to answer one or two difficult questions. Like, how did an obscure group called Diabolic Shroud suddenly become a completely different group called VanillaSex? And how did that group – a *professional* group – manage to break all the rules to win "Battle of the Bands"?'

Initially incredulous, Dan was now white with anger and trying to seize back the initiative.

'April, what is this? Can't you see you're making an exhibition of yourself?'

April just kept on talking.

'. . . a group that you bribed DJ Mike Meen to promote, Dan. A group you once invested heavily in, in your one failure as a rock impresario. You don't like failure, do you Dan? And you don't like people who know too much.

'That's why Marsha Fox decided not to stick around. And that's why—'

'I'm warning you, April, shut up before it's too late.'

'That's why you murdered Diabolic Shroud's ex-drummer, Sven Harlesson. He knew what you were doing, didn't he Dan? Added to which he knew what you were doing to Mersey Roar, and he was going to make sure that every else knew too . . .'

STRANGERS IN THE NIGHT

'This is a malicious lie. You can't prove anything,' snapped Dan Lauren, but nobody was listening to him any more.

The audience was in an uproar, people on their feet and herding towards the stage. Dark figures were moving in from the sides, some in plain clothes, others in uniform. Somewhere in the middle April noticed Marsha Fox, a look of cool jubilation on her face. She and Dan had once been passionate lovers. Strange how swiftly and completely love could turn to hate . . .

You didn't need pillows to enjoy pillowtalk.

Outside the window, a few stars were still sprinkling the lightening sky. The clock ticked round towards four a.m., April's special time of the day. She looked across at Kieran.

'So Kieran, in your fantasy – what happens next?'

'I unbutton your blouse and slip off your bra. It's red satin, my favourite. I kiss your breasts and slide my hand down inside your knickers until I can stroke those beautiful dark curls . . .'

April laughed, low and sexy and seductive.

'And you should be so lucky, Kieran. Now, night owls, the sun's rising and I have to leave you before I turn to dust. Sleep tight and don't let those coffin lids clatter – but before you do, listen to Kieran Harte's show, he needs the ratings.'

Kieran stuck his tongue out at her as she completed the handover and slid over to let him take her place. The seat was deliciously warm from her bare thighs.

215

'Wakey wakey, this is Kieran with your early morning call. Yes, it's the early, early, much *much* too early show on Radio Marina 404 FM, and these young lads are called the Beatles . . .'

He faded up the music and slid his arm round April's waist. She pulled a face.

'Same innovative musical tastes, I see. You might as well have stayed at Mersey Roar.'

'What – and put up with Marsha Fox again? I'd rather put up with you, and that's saying something . . .'

Somewhere in the Irish Sea, between Pier Head and the Isle of Man, a couple of DJs kissed as their pirate radio ship swayed queasily on the early morning swell. It was going to turn into a force eight gale by lunchtime but who cared? They'd weathered the storm; from here on in, everything else would be a pleasure cruise.

Adult Fiction for Lovers from Headline LIAISON

SLEEPLESS NIGHTS	Tom Crewe & Amber Wells	£4.99
THE JOURNAL	James Allen	£4.99
THE PARADISE GARDEN	Aurelia Clifford	£4.99
APHRODISIA	Rebecca Ambrose	£4.99
DANGEROUS DESIRES	J. J. Duke	£4.99
PRIVATE LESSONS	Cheryl Mildenhall	£4.99
LOVE LETTERS	James Allen	£4.99

All Headline Liaison books are available at your local bookshop or newsagent, or can be ordered direct from the publisher. Just tick the titles you want and fill in the form below. Prices and availability subject to change without notice.

Headline Book Publishing, Cash Sales Department, Bookpoint, 39 Milton Park, Abingdon, OXON, OX14 4TD, UK. If you have a credit card you may order by telephone – 01235 400400.

Please enclose a cheque or postal order made payable to Bookpoint Ltd to the value of the cover price and allow the following for postage and packing: UK & BFPO: £1.00 for the first book, 50p for the second book and 30p for each additional book ordered up to a maximum charge of £3.00. OVERSEAS & EIRE: £2.00 for the first book, £1.00 for the second book and 50p for each additional book.

Name ....

Address ....

....

....

If you would prefer to pay by credit card, please complete: Please debit my Visa/Access/Diner's Card/American Express (Delete as applicable) card no:

Signature .... Expiry Date ....